TRUST IN ME

SKYE WARREN

Praise for Trust in Me

"Dark, disturbing, haunting, and beautiful, Skye Warren will take you into the depths of depravity but bring you home, safe in the end."

—Kitty Thomas, author of The Last Girl

"Skye Warren is a true mistress of dark and twisted love stories."

—The Forbidden Bookshelf

Night Owl Top Pick! *"The author plays with metaphors and imagery in a prominent way to express Mia's abuse at the hands the men in her life. This story was literally hard to put down."*

—Night Owl Reviews

"…this author does a really great job at not just showing Mia as a physical whore, but presenting her mental status as a whore is done so well."

—Smexy Books

"It felt like I was reading a much longer book and it was a very intense read. Palpable. Tight."

—Manic Readers

"Mia's character is very well written and as I read the story through her eyes I don't see the mistreated Mia, but a strong young lady who will do whatever it takes to survive and save others."

—Just Erotic Romance Reviews

Author's Foreword

Dear Reader,

I must warn you that this is a disturbing tale, one that starts dark and gets darker. If you are looking for a straight-laced BDSM book, this is not for you. It's intended as a fantasy for those who are as fascinated by erotic pain and consent as I am. The only balm I can offer is that I'm a romantic at heart, and I think that surfaces by the very end.

Yours,
Skye Warren

PROLOGUE

MY STOMACH GROWLED. It pretty much always did that, because my corner was one of the darkest and most dangerous in the city. Not many customers came by. Good corners were run by girls who didn't want to share—or by their pimps. The kind of men who picked me up terrified me, but not as much as pimps did, so I kept working here.

The sweet tang of pot filled the air from two streets down, where homeless guys gathered around a barrel fire. A cat cried out, sending shivers up my spine—until the sound was suddenly cut off.

An ordinary night.

Until a scuffling sound came from the alley. My alley, the one where I took my tricks.

Who's there? And how did they get back there without passing me? But I knew. There was a narrow walkway that ran behind the buildings, connecting all the alleyways. No one ever went back there except the mice—and the cats who chased them.

Except now.

A grunt came from the shadows. From a man or woman? I couldn't tell. Pain sounded the same, all ages and races. Grunts. Screams. Moans. I heard them all on the street. I'd made them all too, one time or another. Pain was a constant here. A currency.

Another grunt. A chill raced over my skin. Someone was getting beaten in that alley. My alley. My fingers gripped the block so hard I felt them bruise—I would break before the old building would. Slowly my eyes adjusted, and I could make out a figure looming over another one slumped against the wall.

Thwack. What was that? A gunshot? Oh God, a gun with a silencer. The tall figure didn't even flinch as the person in front of him slid to the ground and fell sideways.

The man stood and walked away, toward the back walkway.

I bit my lip after he rounded the corner. What if he came back? *Run, Mia. Get out of there.* Except what if the person on the ground was still alive? It might be a working girl like me. Calling the cops was a surefire way to get a target on my back, but if she needed an ambulance, if she needed my help, I would do it.

Doubts ripped through me, tearing me up. I could die if I went in there. I might never come out. But what would be the point of surviving if this is what it cost me? I didn't want to be a person that would see a person bleeding out and walk away. I couldn't live with myself if I didn't try.

After checking that the street was still clear, I crept down the alley and crouched by the figure. Definitely a man, I could see up close. Skinny, with needle tracks down his arms. And definitely dead. I put two fingers to his throat—clammy skin, still warm—and felt no pulse.

Gone.

I glanced up. From the back of the alley, two eyes stared back at me, unblinking in the dark. Oh God. He was there, watching me. I held my breath, bracing for the pain of a bullet. He'd seen me. Even though his face was half hidden, even though I'd never tell the cops, he'd have to kill me now. *I'd seen him.*

A second passed. Another.

My breath hitched. Then I was off like a shot, running toward the street, my cries strangled in my throat. I kept running down the sidewalk. I didn't stop running until I reached the hideaway where I kept my second pair of clothes and my stash of money.

I huddled in that crack in the wall, staring at the night sky, listening to the faraway sirens whiz by.

IT TOOK ME a week to gather the nerve to go back. A week of rotten garbage. A week of fighting the rats for dinner.

The body was gone. Taken away with nothing but a dark stain to mark his place. I felt dizzy looking at it and remembering the glassy stare. No one cared. Not the police. Not the other people on the street. He was just another faceless body—like me. I'd die here too, but not tonight.

Tonight I'd find food.

I stood by the street and tried to look sexy, even though, God, I mostly felt desperate. Some men liked that. A lot of men did.

Moonlight flashed off chrome and glass as a car turned the corner. It seemed to grow longer as it turned. A limo. My heart beat faster.

The shiny black car looked out of place against the crumbling, graffiti-painted concrete. Were they lost? I hoped they didn't stop and ask me for directions. With my luck the neighborhood punks would take the opportunity to jack them and I'd get caught in the crossfire.

Was that what had happened to that guy? No, I'd been around long enough to recognize a hit when I saw one. That had been deliberate. *Murder.*

The limo slid to a stop right in front of me, its engine so quiet all I could hear was the crunch of gravel. I took a step back until I was pressed against the brick wall.

My stomach grumbled, reminding me I could *really* use the money. As in, I might not make it through the night. But the limo was too pretty. Too strange, and in my world, strange was dangerous. And I was still spooked after last week. I braced myself to run, but that would mean turning my back. I learned early not to do that.

The car window rolled down in a smooth glide, revealing a shadowy interior.

"How much?" said a low, masculine voice from inside.

I really need that money.

"Depends what you want," I said, but I was stalling. Was I really going with him? It was always a risk, getting in some stranger's car, but this felt more intense than a ride around the block and a blowjob in an alley. Like I might never see this street corner again.

"Everything," he said.

That didn't reassure me.

But it felt like there was a stampede in my stomach, hunger pains and anxiety rolling together. I couldn't turn him down. I might not get another hit tonight. Fifty cents in my stash wouldn't even buy a soda from the guy at the diner… not unless I sucked him off first.

I figured out how much I'd charge for a blowjob and a fuck. Then I doubled it. "Two hundred."

A low laugh sent chills over my skin. "I think we're going to get along fine," he said.

The back door opened, leaving only a gaping black hole. I was supposed to get inside now. I'd take off my clothes. I'd take off *his* clothes.

If that was all that happened tonight, I could live with that.

But I couldn't stop thinking… why would a guy like this be shopping for a date on this corner? There must be something really wrong with him. What if he wanted kinky stuff?

Or worse?

"The money first," I said. That wasn't standard on the streets, but I wanted it from this guy. Just like the extra money I'd asked for. A little insurance, even though nothing could make this safe.

The rustle of fabric. A hand reached out. I studied that hand like my life depended on it—because it did.

Strong. Masculine. With some sort of white cuff and black jacket, like he was wearing a suit.

He was holding crisp bills, folded once. I snatched them and stared at the money. Two hundred dollar bills. I'd only glimpsed this kind of money in someone's bankroll. I'd never held it. Never had it for myself.

"Coming?" he asked.

I bit my lip, peering inside the car. Pitch black. I couldn't see anything. I'd gotten in a lot of cars. I'd fucked a lot of scary men. I'd survived this long by relying on my instincts, but my instincts told me he was the most dangerous man I'd met.

In the end, I needed this money more than I needed to be safe. Needed *food* more than I needed to be safe. Wasn't it always that way? The human body would survive even when the mind wanted to run. I tucked the bills into my boot.

With a deep breath I stepped into the car and lost my balance for a moment. A hand took my elbow and steadied me. I landed in a seat across from him. He reached for the door handle, and for the briefest moment, the streetlamp lit his face from above, giving him a dark and demonic glow. *The man from the alley!*

Then he closed the door and the limo started moving—with me trapped inside.

Oh God, it was him. He must have recognized me. Hadn't he? Did he know I recognized him too?

This might be a test. He might be waiting for me to mention the murder—or not. If so, I'd never say anything. Not to him, not to the cops. We rode in a silence for seconds… minutes… It felt like forever.

I couldn't take it anymore. "Do you want me to suck—"

"Have you heard of Mateo Bernard?"

My heart started beating faster. Mateo Bernard was known as Pit Bull on the streets. I'd seen him around, and mostly steered clear. He was a scary guy. "No."

"How about Carlos Laguardia?"

Everyone had heard of him. "Why are you asking me this?"

"Information. That's why you're here. Why, did you think I wanted something else?"

My hands tightened into fists. "You know I did."

A hand reached out and grabbed my wrist. I was pulled forward, falling off the seat and almost in his lap. He'd hauled me across the car, and he wasn't even breathing hard. His voice whispered against my temple. "I may take that too. If I want to. When I want to. But first you'll give me the information I need. And after that…"

I whimpered, and he loosened his grip on me. But he didn't let me go.

"After that," he murmured, "you'll give me everything else. Because you're mine. I own you. I bought you for two hundred dollars, understand?"

I was trapped with him, staring at the buildings as they pass by, faster and faster. We picked up speed. I couldn't even say I was worse off in the back of this limo, surrounded by the soft fabric of his clothes and the leather of the seat and the warm skin of his grip.

Did I want to be back on the street? Out in the cold?

My stomach clenched on itself, like it was tearing itself apart. They really might tear me apart tonight if I didn't eat. I had the feeling this guy never went hungry. Never wanted for anything. This could be better for me. I wanted to believe it would better. As long as…

"I understand," I whispered. He'd bought my silence, I understood that too. "But… don't hurt me."

He sounded almost regretful when he said, "I can't promise you that. But I'll promise you this. Whatever happens, I won't let you die."

His arms around me were an embrace, but his words—they felt like a threat.

CHAPTER ONE

"**C**OME, SLUT." His words dragged my body across the floor, invisible chains. I hated him for calling me that way. I hated myself more for going to him. And I went the way I knew he wanted me to—crawling. A layer of grime covered the concrete floor of the warehouse, but it was only fitting to crawl through muck. This whole game was dirty, and so was I.

Carlos looked down at me from his seat with a half-smile. The guy next to him was speaking in low, urgent tones, but I had his attention.

Other whores might try coy smiles or a flash of cleavage, but if you really knew *El Jefe*—and, unfortunately, I did—then you knew all you had to do was drop to his feet. I knew what he wanted and how he liked it, knowledge born of years of training. As long as I behaved, he wouldn't kill me. I craved the release of death, but I was too well trained to earn it.

I reached his leather shoes and waited. The same Italian leather shoes that had kicked me only recently, but they weren't a danger to me now. Carlos didn't like to get too messy when he had guests. Even though I didn't like performing, I could be glad this new guy was around today. Then again, I'd probably have to service him next.

Carlos unzipped his pants.

The guy sucked in a quiet breath, as if we'd shocked him.

That wouldn't stop Carlos. He wasn't an exhibitionist. He was a sadist, and the only thing better than causing someone physical pain was causing emotional discomfort. Every pinch was designed to humiliate, every blow to subjugate. *You're not worthy*, they said, and I lapped up every blow to my shrunken ego like the masochist I'd learned to be.

Eagerly, I leaned forward and sucked the head of his cock with my mouth. Eager because delays were only an excuse to punish me later, and Carlos was nothing if not creative, and extreme, in his punishments. The whips, the knives, the *cage*. I shuddered.

His cock was musky today, but not urine-tinged—I could be thankful for that, too. Finding things to be thankful for kept me sane. It could always be worse. It had been.

I worked my tongue in a swirl and laved under the tip of his cock. Carlos grunted.

It was almost funny, the way the guy next to him stuttered a few starts, as if unsure if he should continue talking to the infamous *El Jefe* while he was getting his dick sucked. I hadn't gotten a good look at the guy, just a brief glimpse of jeans and a black t-shirt. Mostly I noticed a big, strong male body. That was enough. Maybe some girls got turned on. I just got scared. It wasn't about weakness or strength. This was pure survival instinct.

"Go on, Martinez," Carlos said gruffly. "Continue."

Martinez started talking again, something about deliveries and security. Carlos put his hands over my ears. Not so I couldn't hear the conversation. He never worried about trusting me because he didn't think I was smart enough to do anything about it. That was my one victory, however small.

No, his hands over my ears were a warning. If I didn't do it on my own, he'd shove my face down so I couldn't breathe. I could deep throat before I came here, but two years with Carlos had beaten the skill right out of me. He didn't train me to do better, he beat me to do worse, until my nerves manifested in performance that could be punished. He loved to hold my face down so I couldn't breathe, until even a shallow blowjob filled me with panic.

I pushed my head down, forcing his cock to slide along my tongue and sink deep in my throat. *Breathe*, I told myself firmly, *and whatever you do, don't gag.* Gagging didn't make him angry, it made him horny. The sadistic kind of horny that led to worse things.

I pulled back. His fingers tightened in my hair, not letting me go too far. Then I plunged down again. And again. Over and over I took him deep in my throat, still breathing, not gagging. So far, so good.

Martinez, though—damn. I glanced up, trying to see the man, but Carlos's arm blocked my view. All I could see was a strong jaw obscured by a few days' scruff and a low-pulled cap. It couldn't be him. Martinez was a common enough name. He was long gone, but the memories rattled in their cage.

Hey, little girl. Whatcha doing out here?
Nothin'.
You should do nothin' inside then. It's not safe out here.

The man in my memories hadn't known it wasn't safe inside either. Or maybe he had known, but pretended he didn't. He wouldn't have been the only one to turn away. The long-buried memories escaped their tight confines, flooding my mind. They had no place in my life now. Every whore had a sob story, but no one wanted to think about it—least of all the whore.

Maybe Carlos could tell I was distracted because he clamped his hand behind my head and shoved it all the way down. His cock popped into my throat with a sickening gurgle. I worked at a swallow, but I couldn't help it—I gagged. Panic swept over me, tossing me, drowning me. *Can't breathe, let me go.*

I forced my arms to remain by my sides, where he wanted them. I'd rather pass out than suffer a punishment. At least, my mind knew that. My body squirmed and jerked in tiny pleas for mercy. Finally, thankfully, he pulled back my head just enough to pop his cock out of my throat. I sucked in deep breaths through my nose—

grateful, so grateful—until he shoved it back in again. It shouldn't have been a surprise, but somehow it was, every time. The ache, the burn, the horror that I'd let this happen to me yet again.

His cock filled my awareness, until all I smelled or felt or could think of was the thick flesh in my mouth. When it was in, I was in pain, I couldn't breathe, I must not move. When it was out, the sweet rush of air breathed consciousness back into me.

His movements became jerky. His hand tightened painfully in my hair. I imagined his face pale and tight as it was right before he came, but my nose was buried in his crotch and my eyes were full of tears.

He yanked my head far enough back that only the tip of his cock was in before he spewed his load into my mouth. I knew he wanted me to get the full impact of the spray, the full salty flavor of his come that wouldn't have happened if he'd been deep. Even swallowing was degrading, a voluntary act.

Unlike other men I'd seen, and the few I'd serviced, Carlos barely ever made a sound when he came. Mostly he was silent, tense and contained even in his crisis. When he released me, I staggered back onto the floor. He wouldn't hurt me, not so soon after he'd come, so I lay there, sprawled and heaving, waiting for my eyes to dry and my breath to catch.

When the shadowed office came into focus, I looked away from the sight of Carlos tucking himself into his pants and peeked at the other guy. Martinez. Light brown hair, almost a sandy blond that belied his surname, and a strong jaw. He looked up at me. Blue eyes seared mine like a blinding summer sun.

Oh God. I knew him. It wasn't a coincidence. He was *my* Martinez, though the ownership was only in my delusions. Tyler Martinez, my childhood neighbor, the golden boy of the *barrio*. I'd had a massive crush on him. He'd barely noticed me, though in his defense, he was older than me, which was a big deal when I was twelve and he was eighteen. Then he'd left for the military, I heard, and I never saw him again. Until now.

Those blue eyes widened as he looked at me, mirroring my own shock. His lips formed my name, *Mia*, but thank God, no sound emerged. I couldn't believe he recognized me. It had been—what?—ten years. I couldn't believe he even remembered me.

I must look different, all grown up. And—oh God— I'd just sucked a guy off in front of him. Not just any guy, a crime boss with a penchant for whores. Tyler knew who I was, *what* I was. My stomach knotted, trying to turn my body inside out. I wanted to die. My self-hatred, which I would have thought peaked years ago, climbed another notch. Bad enough that this was my life, bad enough this had *always* been my life, but for *him* to know, for him to have seen me this way, was too much.

"Here, cunt, show our new friend some hospitality," Carlos said.

No. I don't want to. That thought distracted me for a second. Since when did I say no, even in my mind?

Somewhere deep inside, did I still think I had the right?

I met Tyler's gaze again and was snapped back to reality. The life where, no, I didn't have a choice. And where, worst of all, he looked chagrined by the thought of a blowjob from me. More than that, he looked disgusted, leaning away, not meeting my eyes. Jesus, there was a blow to the self-esteem I didn't even know I had. I deserved his revulsion. I knew that better than him, but it hurt to see the eyes I had once longed for, dreamed of, judging my scantily clad body.

Pain slammed through my side. I gasped for air. Those boots again. Damn, I hadn't been watching. Too distracted. "Come on," Carlos was saying, "what's taking you so long, you stupid bitch?"

Every cell of my body screamed to run. I would rather die, rather suffer any punishment, than touch Tyler as a whore. I'd gladly pleasure him of my own free will, but not like this. Tears filled my eyes. At least Carlos would think they were from the pain. I'd never been able to hold them back, which was probably the reason why I was Carlos's favorite girl. His only girl.

I would have to comply. Even if I decided to leave for good, I'd have to wait and do it when I was alone. Plan an escape. If I balked now, Carlos would just beat the shit out of me until I obeyed. Or until I died. Besides, I had a purpose here. If I could help a single girl escape *this*, it was worth it. My dignity had dried up years ago, but other women still had a chance.

With my mouth filled with the bitter taste of Carlos's

semen and my own self-loathing, I shuffled toward Tyler. He shifted on the seat as I approached. I knew he didn't want this. It was clear in his eyes, his posture, as if I was attacking him and he was trapped. How ironic.

I almost wanted Tyler to refuse. *Almost.*

If he refused me, Carlos would make me pay the price, and it would be dear. Which would I prefer, to make myself a whore of my childhood crush or to suffer unspeakable pain?

But it wasn't my choice to make after all, because Tyler said, "Stop."

I froze, waiting for it, hoping, dreading.

"You don't like her?" Carlos asked. His voice held a warning note, not to Tyler, but to me. "Let us seal our partnership. I can bring in another girl if this one doesn't please you."

"No," Tyler said, his voice strangled. "I...like her. She's good. I was just thinking I wanted more time with her, maybe a room."

My breath caught. Mostly I hated the idea. But a small part of me, the part of me that was still a childish little girl and hopeful, loved it. As if this could be the erotic coupling of my dreams, a shiny peel to disguise the rotting core of human slavery.

"Ah, privacy," Carlos mused. "You'd like to play with her alone."

We waited. I didn't know what Tyler's agenda was, whether he truly wanted me or if it was just a ploy to get out of a blowjob from a dirty whore, but I held my breath for the verdict.

"That is fine," Carlos said lightly, as if he hadn't just answered my prayers and doomed me at the same time.

Tyler's breath released along with mine.

"Take him to my bedroom," Carlos said. "Tyler is my good friend, so please him well." *Or else.*

I stood up and straightened my skimpy halter and short skirt, as if I had any dignity left, and led Tyler from the room. Neither of us spoke as we moved through the barren halls. Not even as we passed a couple of the men, who leered but knew better than to mess with me when I had Tyler at my side.

Once inside Carlos's room, I studied it through Tyler's eyes. Shiny surfaces and gaudy mirrors left no doubt as to what sort of acts they normally reflected. The leather wall paneling and black silk sheets cinched the deal—this room was for sex.

Tyler whirled on me. I could tell he was going to say something, ask something, so I kissed him. It was only to stop him, but I enjoyed myself anyway. Be thankful where you can, that was my motto, and I was thankful for this. His lips were soft and warm, and shockingly, he responded to my kiss, pressing his lips back and tangling his tongue with mine. He wasn't chilly or slimy. He didn't taste bad.

When we parted, we were both panting. With my lips only an inch from his, I breathed, "There's cameras."

His eyes widened for a second, then he nodded slightly. His arms came around me and pulled my body into his. He understood. Don't act like we know each other, don't say anything incriminating. From the moment we'd pretended not to know each other, it was me and Tyler against Carlos.

How had he come to work with Carlos? How had he ended up back in the old neighborhood? I had imagined him somewhere with a great family and a good job. I didn't like that he was back here in Shitsville, mixed up with dangerous people.

"So Carlos just gives his girlfriend to anyone who asks?" he asked in a low tone.

From somewhere deep I pulled a careless laugh. "I'm not his girlfriend."

He raised one eyebrow. "That's not how it looked to me."

God, the innocence. He really wasn't cut out to be working with a guy like Carlos. "I'm whatever he tells me to be," I said, infusing myself with a sexiness I didn't feel. "I'm a whore."

Tyler's eyes darkened. "Why?"

"A girl's gotta eat," I said lightly. It wasn't even a lie. That had been the reason once. I stroked a finger down my neck because it seemed like something a whore would do, and because I wanted to.

His fingertips tightened on my hips, and he shook me slightly. "Damn it, Mia."

I sharpened my gaze in warning.

"Isn't that what you said your name was?" he murmured.

Then he kissed me. It was an act, like my kiss had been, but just as quickly it became real. He tasted me, caressed me, and I'd never had it like this. I'd never been kissed by a man who treated me gently, who knew who I was, and at least for the moment, wanted me anyway. I'd never been kissed by a man I liked. I'd never liked a man that wasn't Tyler. I didn't deserve it but I took it anyway, which made me just as bad as Carlos.

"How long do we have?" he asked between breaths.

"As long as you want," came the automatic reply.

He nipped at my lips. Not the right answer.

"Maybe an hour," I whispered. Any longer and Carlos would get anxious. Much less and he'd know I hadn't properly pleased Tyler. "Are you going to…?" *Fuck me.*

"I don't know," he muttered. "I wasn't counting on cameras. What happens if we just kiss? Make out?"

Pain. Tears. Blood. "Nothing," I said. "Do what you want."

He scowled.

I widened my eyes. "What?"

"You're not as good a liar as you think you are. What happens if we don't fuck?" he asked.

His voice held a command, and that, at least, I was used to. Damn. I didn't know if I could trust this guy, but somewhere deep inside I already did.

"I'll get in trouble." I shook my head to show him it didn't matter. The last thing I wanted to do was pressure him into sex.

"What kind of trouble?" he asked. When I didn't

answer, he pulled me tighter against him. I went limp, a reflex. "What happens when you get in trouble?"

My throat tightened. I couldn't tell him, couldn't explain about the pain. The terror, the agony.

"Christ," he said. "Tell me."

I shook my head. "It's nothing." *It's everything. Please, just fuck me.*

"If he hurts you then why…?"

I knew what he'd meant to say. Why did I stay, then? The irony was that I had the same question for him. Working for a guy like Carlos had "bad idea" written all over it. Why would anyone want to stay in this shithole if he had the option to leave? But both of us were here. The better question was, what was holding us prisoners?

CHAPTER TWO

TYLER SIGHED, RESIGNED. "Okay. Come on."

And really, isn't that just what every girl wants to hear from a guy agreeing to fuck her? But I wasn't like every girl. This was a job, that was all.

He led me to the bed and pulled me down with him. But I didn't want him, not like this. I didn't want him to have sex with me, not if he didn't want me. I only remained here to protect those girls from forced sex, from rape. I couldn't do the same thing to Tyler, not even to spare myself pain.

"Wait," I said. "You don't have to do this. Please don't."

"I have to," he said, his teeth gritted.

This was all wrong. "You don't want this," I whispered.

He pulled my hand to his jeans where I felt his hardness pushing against the zipper. "Does this feel like I don't want it?"

I already knew the body had nothing to do with the mind. "No," I said. "I can tell you don't. It doesn't matter about me."

He pushed me onto my back and loomed over me.

"This is happening. Are you going to fight me?"

I shook my head. No, I wouldn't—*couldn't*—fight Tyler, not ever. No matter how I pledged my allegiance to Carlos, I couldn't help but fight and resist every time he hurt me. With Tyler, it hurt just to be near him, but I'd endure it, if only to pretend a few minutes more.

He kissed me again, and it was almost real. Like a real kiss between two people having sex, as if I knew what that felt like. Both of us were doing this for business or to avoid pain or whatever reason, but none having to do with passion or pleasure. Still, I felt a long-buried stirring of passion. And, too, I felt pleasure as his lips molded over mine and his body lowered.

The weight of him, the heat of him, was delicious. Somehow I felt safe with him, which was a stupid error to make after working so hard and so long to be careful. He was working with Carlos—I couldn't forget that. If Carlos ever found out I was double-crossing him, he wouldn't kill me. He would keep me alive and make me wish I were dead.

Tyler's hands found my breasts and easily slipped under the small halter top. He looked down at my breast in his hand. I knew I had beautiful breasts. Not because they looked beautiful to me—I hated the sight of them—but because I'd been told so. From very young, I'd been told how pretty they were—large, despite my lanky body, and pale with dark, hardened tips.

He groaned, just staring. "So beautiful."

I hated that he said that, that he noticed what all the

other men had noticed, that he was like them after all. At the same time, I almost preened. At least I had pleased him in some way. One of these days my contradictions would tear me apart.

His fingertip, blunt and rough, traced from the top of the slope to the tip.

"Why are you doing this?" he muttered, and it didn't sound like he was talking to me but to himself.

Why *was* he doing this? Why did he need to get mixed up with Carlos? It would only end badly for Tyler. I had seen enough of Carlos's business partners disappear to know that. God, but I didn't want to think that Tyler would even want to be involved. Carlos had lots of different businesses, but they were all bad—drugs, guns. And my personal crusade, my curse, human trafficking. Which was Tyler involved in?

"You shouldn't be here," slipped out on a moan.

"I know," he said, still mesmerized by my hated breasts.

"It isn't right." Why couldn't he see? I wanted him to be good, but if he couldn't do that, then at least I wanted him to be safe.

"I can't stop," he said. Then he looked up at me. "I won't hurt you."

Too late for that. "Just do it," I said. *Get it over with, never let it end.*

He bent his head and kissed my nipple. Not sucked, not bit, just kissed. "I shouldn't." He bared my other breast and kissed that nipple. "Want you."

Pins pricked behind my eyes. It was sweet, too sweet. "No," I whispered.

"Shh," he said. "It's okay." His hands caressed my breasts as his erection pressed against me below, fitting perfectly.

I needed it to be over before I did something embarrassing, like cry or orgasm. I drew on every seduction I'd ever attempted, which wasn't many. I wasn't used to enticing men to have sex with me. Usually they wanted it badly enough to pay me or force me, and if they didn't, I had no desire to change their minds about that. But for him, I would.

I squirmed first, just an awkward jerk of my body, but he groaned and pushed his hips onto me. I eased his shirt up and sucked in a breath of my own at the feel of his hard body. I'd had sex with strong men before, big men. Carlos, though getting older, was no slouch. He couldn't be in his business or he'd be dead, but his muscles were like all his power—bulky. Powerful in a domineering way. And whenever he'd given me to one of his "business partners" he'd been like Carlos. A thick, beefy man.

Tyler, though, had lean, ropey muscles. Not like a bully, like an athlete. Long contours defined his back and deep ridges stacked his stomach. It was a scary kind of strength, that he could use to hurt me so precisely. It wouldn't be a careless, blunt-force pain with him, but precise. Assuming he was into pain. In my experience, all guys were, if they thought they could get away with it.

I reached down and rubbed his erection through his jeans. His whole body tensed, like he'd just stuck his finger in an electric socket, but he let me. He let me touch him, explore his shape as he held himself above me in a parody of a push-up. A whim overtook me, and I reached up and kissed his nipple, just as he'd done mine. So sweet, so strange.

I swallowed hard. What was I doing? Making this count as if it meant something? God, I was a fucking idiot. I was a *whore*. Not even Tyler's whore. I belonged to Carlos, who had given me to Tyler for a quick fuck. This only meant something in my own mind. I'd meant nothing to Tyler before today, just some distant memory of a dumb little girl, and his opinion of me would be even worse after this.

I fell back onto the bed. The silken sheets were cool against my heated skin, the cold fingers of reality cradling my weary body. I waited, waited for the inevitable. That was the good thing about my profession, that I could mostly just wait around and get fucked. Sure, sometimes I had to suck or thrust or something, but that was only my body. And my body, bless its dirty, shameful heart, had an auto-pilot function.

He'd undone his pants. My skirt had flared up at my hips, exposing my bare sex. A wrapper tore and then he fitted his covered dick into me.

It was all happening so fast, thankfully. Whatever monster lay at the bottom of the lake had dragged me under, and I could only watch the proceedings with a drugged sort of detachment.

His hands on my body. His weight pressing down. His cock inside me. A sharp intake of breath as he entered. It was all about him and what he did to me, and not about me. It wasn't about what I felt.

It was his sounds that distracted me. The silence of a breath held as he withdrew slightly. Then a low groan as he plunged deep. The rustle of silk.

His harsh breathing blew across my face, waking me from slumber like a kiss from a prince. Small wet sucks marked each stroke, filled the room, and reflected back to me in stereo. The shuffle of skin against fabric, the rasp of his stubble against my shoulder, his soft grunt as he pushed his way inside. They were timeless sounds, ancient sounds, but they were new to me.

I'd never listened to sex before, never wanted to. I'd always tuned them out, but now they beat at my eardrums, demanding my attention. What was he doing to me?

Then he held himself above me, inside me, and released a masculine sound of pleasure. More a vibration than a sound, and it filled me, wound its way through me like smoke in a glass.

He pulled out of me and none too soon, collapsing beside me on the slick, damp sheets.

"Christ, Mia," he blew out on a breath. "Fucking Christ."

Did that mean he liked me? Why did I care?

It made me angry all of a sudden, the contrast. Today he slung his naked thigh over my legs, his hand over my ribs while his thumb swept the undercurve of my breast. Today he swore at me, and I didn't know what it meant.

Ten years ago, he'd held himself apart. He'd held himself away from me, and I'd thought he had deserved that higher position, and probably he did, but I still hated it. The memory came rushing back to me. Ten years and so little had changed really.

Suddenly I was there on that sticky summer night…

"Hey, little girl," he'd said, hanging his thumbs in his jeans pockets. That's what he called me, even though he knew my name. "Whatcha doing out here?"

I flicked a pebble across the lawn. "Nothin'."

He smiled at me with those beautiful blue eyes. "You should do nothin' inside then. It's not safe out here."

I looked across the row of backyards. All of them were small and stark, but ours was the worst, filled with trash and weeds. It wasn't particularly safe, no. Sometimes I'd hear a crash or a scream at night, but I knew better than to go outside and see what it was. It wasn't safe inside either, not for me.

Maybe I had some crazy idea that he would care. Maybe I thought he would protect me. "I don't want to go back in," I said. "Not ever."

"Aww." He sat down next to me on the old semi tire, giving me a nudge. "It can't be as bad as all that."

But he didn't understand, he didn't *know*. No one knew. Even though he lived right next door, right there, he had no idea what went on in my house.

"It's horrible," I told him with the kind of complete honesty only a child can muster. "Like hell."

He frowned. "You shouldn't use that word."

"Everyone else uses it," I said with a petulance that should already have worked its way out of my system, considering the circumstances. But even then I'd felt safe with Tyler. Something about his quiet intensity, his regard when no one else noticed me, made me feel that when he was next to me, no one could hurt me. Not that everyone hurt me. Only a parent can really hurt a twelve-year-old girl. I had one parent, a father.

"Maybe everyone does," he said, "but you shouldn't. You're still a kid. It isn't right."

Of course I knew I was a kid. I knew that an eighteen-year-old guy about to leave home had no business at all with a twelve-year-old girl with a crush. He didn't speak to me often above a quick wave and how-do when he passed me on the street. I should have been grateful for that much. I should have known not to ask for more. It would only lead to disappointment.

"Please, Tyler. Can't you take me somewhere? Just take me away. I'll go anywhere."

His frown deepened. "Mia, what's wrong?"

I love you. The sound of the screen door opening screeched across the words I'd meant to say, scratching them out.

"Mia, get your ass inside," my dad called.

I hesitated, still delusional enough to think Tyler

might stop him, might help me.

"*Now*, Mia," my dad said.

I looked up at Tyler. His face was dark as he looked my father. Then he turned to me and nodded toward the house. "Go on," he said gently. Just two words spoken softly, but they shattered me. No, Tyler wasn't going to help. Tyler wasn't going to love me. No one would.

I ran inside the house, tripping blindly through my tears.

I should have been immune after that, but that was just wishful thinking. The knife that had stabbed my heart twisted as I crouched inside the kitchen, listening.

"Mr. Campbell," Tyler was saying, "I don't mean to tell you how to run your family, but I wonder if something is going on with Mia."

"You don't mean to tell me, but you do, eh? No one asked your opinion."

"I know, sir, but she seemed mighty upset. Maybe if you—"

"She was upset because you was harassing her. What's a grown boy got to do with a young girl, anyhow? Looks suspect to me. Maybe I should go calling the Army, let them know what kind of recruit they'll be getting."

"That's ridiculous," Tyler said, his voice tight. "Look, I wasn't trying to upset you. I don't really know her but it just seemed like she might be going through a rough patch. Like children do. That's all."

My father yelled out a couple more threats, and Tyler

left me to my fate. The words replayed through my mind. *That's ridiculous. I don't really know her. Like children do.*

All of it was true, of course, which only made it worse. I clutched the pain of his words like a security blanket. Even when my father came back inside and locked the doors, chased me up to my room, and worked out his anger at Tyler on my little girl body, the pain protected me.

For years it had protected me, blanketed me, shielded me from the full assault of my choices or lack of choices. Now Tyler was back in my life in the worst possible way, and he wanted to strip away my pain, layer by layer. With his words and his kisses and his *sounds*, he pierced the veil that had been my survival. What would I have left when he was done with me?

Even when he'd recovered his breath, he held me tight in a slumped embrace, in a parody of a post-coitus cuddle. "Mia, why are you here? Do you need help? Do you need money or something?" His words came low and solemn, with eyes so concerned.

I had to get rid of him.

And anyway, what could I tell him—the truth? That after he left to go live his life, I was trapped in my father's house for six long days of the hell I'd tried to tell him about? That when I'd run away from home, starving and scared, I'd survived for years on the street, only to be taken in by Carlos? And that, despite the fact that I owed him my life and my loyalty, I was planning to betray

Carlos just to give those girls another chance at life, a chance I'd never had and never would? For all I knew, Tyler was part of the trafficking business. For all I knew, he was Carlos's supplier. There was no way I could trust him.

So I forced myself to laugh. "Shit, Tyler, don't get all serious on me just because you had a good fuck. I like what I do. It's easy and the pay's great."

He considered me, doubted me. He was older, more filled out, weathered, but with his blue eyes frowning at me, he looked like the eighteen-year-old boy from all those years ago more than ever.

He hadn't believed me way back then, at least not enough to stay and help. So what did it matter if he made the offer now? Too little and way too late.

Looking him right in the eyes, I said, "I'm a whore through-and-through, and that's what I'll be until the day that I die."

And I let him look for the lie in my face, because I knew he wouldn't find it. That last bit, at least, was the truth.

CHAPTER THREE

T HE DIAMOND EARRINGS winked at me in the mirror, chains of silver and jewels. At least make-up covered up my sallow skin and sunken eyes. Too much thinking and not enough sleep over the past week had taken their toll on my appearance, my only commodity.

Carlos hadn't complained, though. Not earlier that day when I'd sucked him off from under his desk while he was on his conference call.

"Next week? That's a whole month early," Carlos snapped into the phone while his dick jerked in my mouth.

A tinny voice answered him, garbled words about screwing the pooch and timetables.

"That's ridiculous," Carlos said. "Moving the delivery up makes us more susceptible, not less."

The voice grew louder, buzzing from the phone with furor and reprimand. I knew it grated on Carlos that they used a voice modulator with him, that they didn't even trust him enough to have a conversation. Around here, Carlos was a big fucking deal. But these guys were Russian mafia—the real deal.

Carlos shifted in his seat, holding my head steady.

"Look, maybe I can move some things around, but it's going to be tight." His voice had turned softer, almost obsequious, something I'd never heard from him before. It was like sucking the cock of a stranger.

After that Carlos had put me in my cage, where my eyes had glazed over but my ears had listened intently for any useful information about the shipment. Human trafficking, something at once both horrifying and painfully commonplace. But this I could do something about. For once, I had power. Or I would, once I ferreted out the information.

I was told to dress nice, that we were having a guest. Although it was a work meeting, Carlos had ordered a fancy dinner. I didn't know who it was, just that the guy meeting us tonight was heading up security for the drop. Perfect.

Outside my room, I ran into Trunk. No one knew his real name, but he was built like a tree trunk, and was almost as quiet as one. He caught me by the arm as I passed.

"Can I talk to you?" he said, low and gruff.

The men weren't supposed to touch me. It was against Carlos's rules. But they knew they could get away with it, at least a little bit, without me complaining. After all, if I whined to Carlos every time one of them roughed me up, Carlos would probably take his anger out on me.

"I got nothing to say," I said, trying not to think of how the last time Trunk had spoken to me, he'd also hurt me. He'd fucked me, and I hoped he knew better than to try it now.

Trunk grunted and pushed me back inside.

"Big stuff is going down," he said when we were inside and the door shut. "It's not safe for you."

"What—is that a threat?" My voice wavered embarrassingly. What kind of whore was afraid of sex?

"No." His cold eyes seemed almost sympathetic. "Keep your head down and stay out of it."

"Why the hell are you telling me this?"

"Just do it or you'll fucking get hurt."

Then he was gone, and I was leaning against the inside of the door. Well, it sure as hell had sounded like a threat. And from a guy who'd barely ever said two words to me, except when Carlos had let him…I forced my mind away.

It was a little early, but Carlos didn't take well to waiting, so I wandered downstairs. The cook had already set out a few hors d'oeuvres platters. I appreciated that Carlos had servants to do the cooking and the serving and the cleaning, at least in the residential areas. Technically I was a servant, too, to do the fucking.

I actually liked cooking, but it would have felt too domestic to do it for Carlos. Too reminiscent of the kind of life I'd never have.

Male voices echoed from the hallway. I stood on my too-high heels and smoothed my black sheath dress. But I recognized one of the voices—Tyler. *Shit.*

I hadn't seen him since that day he'd met with Carlos—and fucked me. It had been a week. I hoped never to see him again, that his business wouldn't require another meeting or maybe that Tyler would call off the whole thing. And I prayed that whatever he was involved in, it wasn't this. None of Carlos's businesses were any good, so maybe it was hypocritical to even have a preference, but I did.

Even now, disillusioned though I was, *realist* that I was, I didn't want to think that Tyler could be involved in human trafficking. But apparently he was involved. And right in the thick of things, head of security. *Fuck.*

It was just one more layer, one more obstacle. I would have to betray Carlos, which would have been bad enough and difficult enough, but now I'd be betraying Tyler, too. I wasn't too worried about Carlos. He was like a cockroach—he could survive even a nuclear disaster. Probably turn a nice buck, too. When I broke up the trafficking bit, he'd lose some money and some credibility. That would be it. But Tyler, shit. If he was running security, he'd be right *there*. He might get caught. He might get killed. And it would all be my fault.

I smoothed my face in a well-practiced move as they came into the room. Tyler's icy blue eyes ran over my body and then away. He was cold to me after I'd given him my spiel about once-a-whore-always-a-whore. Probably I'd torn down some of his illusions about quiet little girls not growing up into dirty prostitutes, but whatever. He was one to judge, considering what kind of business he was in.

I played the serene hostess, offering food or service, but not speaking much. That's what Carlos wanted. I was a prop, like his Rolex or the antique furniture. Expensive things belonged to powerful men.

I sat between them, touching both of them while they touched me back. I was the link between them, the conduit. It wasn't sexual between them, not like that. It was more like a fist bump, mob boss style.

Tyler put his hand on my bare thigh, too high to be anything innocent. "How long has she been with you?"

He spoke over me, across me, to Carlos. The dismissal was obvious and no less painful because I already knew what he was.

"A few years now," Carlos said. "She's a loyal one. And pretty, no?"

"Yes," Tyler said, stroking my leg, higher, higher. "Very pretty. She stays with you all the time?"

Carlos laughed. "So she did please you. Yes, she stays with me. Why, are you interested in a rental?"

"Maybe," Tyler said.

Carlos ran his knuckles across my breast. "Normally I wouldn't consider such a thing. I like to keep her near. She is good stress relief. But for you? Well, we'll see."

I fumed inside. My anger and pain and humiliation curled and coiled over my skin until they threatened to strangle me. I was used to being a whore. I was used to being passed around, to being a toy and not a person. But not to Tyler. I wasn't used to being treated as less than human by Tyler and I never would be.

It was my fault. I'd tried to put him off the whole humanitarian bit by convincing him I was truly a whore. Apparently I'd convinced him since he was now content to treat me like one.

Tyler's fingers nudged my thigh to the side. I let it fall open. The short black skirt rode even higher, just barely covering the bare skin at the center. He inched his fingers up until they touched my sensitive flesh. I wanted to gasp, to squirm, but instead I went deathly still.

Let him have my body. It wasn't worth much anyway.

Tyler fingered me, gently at least, as his mouth found my neck. Jesus, he was horny as hell. He'd certainly gotten over his reticence since last time. Maybe even that had been an act, pretending like he was reluctant, like he only fucked me because Carlos would punish me otherwise. A guy who participated in trafficking wouldn't exactly value a woman, especially not one like me.

But, traitor that my body was, his ministrations started to affect me. Wetness coated his fingers, but that was a good thing. It kept me safe, kept my pussy from getting torn apart by invading fingers and cocks and other things. Little sparks of pleasure appeared, taunting my anger at Tyler. I wasn't really mad at Tyler. I was mad at myself. How could I let myself be pleasured by him?

Conversationally, with his fingers in my pussy, Tyler said, "How often do you pass her around?"

I clenched around his fingers, but not in pleasure.

Carlos's hands, which had been stroking my breast, tightened painfully. Didn't Tyler know who he was dealing with?

"Whenever I want. She's mine," Carlos said. I'd expected more anger, but that was probably coming. He seemed as surprised as I that Tyler would speak to him so disrespectfully.

"I would think…" Tyler trailed off thoughtfully.

"Yes?" Carlos clipped out.

"I would think if you had a girl who served you well, you wouldn't want to share her."

Carlos's fingers dug into my breast. My hips jerked in a silent plea for mercy against Tyler's hand.

"Weren't you just the one asking to borrow her?" Carlos said in a silken tone. "And now you complain about my methods? But let's not forget. Your area of expertise is on keeping the bitches fenced in. Me? I have years of training whores like her."

Tyler shrugged, unconcerned with the beast in the room. "I want her, sure. I could take her off your hands even, if you were looking to sell."

Carlos narrowed his eyes.

"I'm thinking of expanding," Tyler explained. "Building a personal line. I could learn a lot from a guy like you. And she'd be a great starter piece."

Carlos eyes widened briefly, which for him was practically preening. "You can purchase one from the shipment. A fresh one."

"Sure." Tyler shrugged. "But that one's getting older,

hmm? You could get a nice young one to use your experience on. But this one, already well behaved, would set an example for other girls I purchased."

It was a new experience for me, being negotiated over while I was in the room. Disappointment seared me, because I'd thought, or hoped, that Tyler could be different. He'd asked if I needed help, if I needed money or something, and I thought that meant that he was a nice guy. Or maybe that our history meant something, however small. But here he was, ready to establish me as head whore on his new little harem. Fabulous.

"I'll think about it." Carlos stood. He dug his fingers into my hair, yanked me up beside him, and marched me off into his office. Before I knew it, I was bent over his desk, getting slammed into from behind. He was turned on, but it wasn't from me. It was Tyler's words that had done it, every covetous word as much a stroke to his cock as his ego.

At least my pussy was ready to take him this time, I told myself. At least I wasn't dry.

I'd had all kinds of sex. Quick sex, painful sex, humiliating sex, but this was the least sex-like sex I'd ever had. It wasn't about lust, it was about power. Not even ownership, which implies a certain regard for the object, even pride. This was more like getting pissed in the face by a dog. He didn't care about his territory, he just didn't want anyone else to have it.

Carlos's hand tangled in my hair, curling me back in an unnatural arc as he whispered in my ear, "Yes, I taught you well, didn't I, whore? Making the other guys want you. Fucking whore."

His fingers groped at me, grabbed at me, mastered me before I'd even given a thought to rebellion. I'd known this evening would include sex, but I'd thought I'd have a break at least, some time to pretend I was a regular girl and not this. Stupid, really.

As my ass tilted back, he rammed in deep, too deep. He bottomed out, hitting my cervix and I couldn't help the whimpers that escaped. Then with a harsh expulsion of air, he came inside me. *Thank God.*

He slipped out of me wetly, then fell back across his desk chair.

"Go on," he said, slurred. "Entertain him. Show him how well I trained you."

I'd expected Tyler to be on the couch where we left him. He was across the room, and that was okay, maybe he was wandering around or maybe he'd gotten some of the food that was laid out. He didn't turn as I approached, too engrossed in something. Maybe I should have been scared, maybe that was the point of the whole charade, to put me off of him, but I was curious. Even knowing what I knew, everything about him fascinated me—the smell of his aftershave, the soft hair on his arm, the way a smile flickered on his face without him seeming to move a muscle.

So when I reached his back and he still hadn't noticed me, I peeked around his arm. It was a stupid move, just like thinking smart-ass thoughts, the kind of thing that could get you killed. But I did it, and what I saw was enough to make me regret my brashness.

Tyler was holding what I immediately recognized to be Carlos's phone. It was a popular kind of smartphone in a black case, so maybe it could have been Tyler's, except I knew it wasn't. The way he was holding it, kind of shielding it from view, his fingers hesitant on the tiny buttons would have been enough. But the little black cable that stuck out of it, some kind of wire, proved the whole thing. He was downloading data or uploading a virus or *something*, but it wouldn't be good.

A sharp intake of breath ripped through the room, and I realized it had come from me. He whirled on me, and I watched with morbid fascination as emotions flashed across his face. Fear, anger, frustration—things at once familiar and foreign. Resignation, that one I knew well.

The heavy clod of footsteps signaled Carlos's return. Tyler yanked the cord from the phone and slid it onto the console table. The cord disappeared, presumably into Tyler's pockets. His eyes met mine, daring me to say anything, asking me not to.

Carlos gave me a smirk. "Hungry, chica?"

He was always nicest after an rough fuck.

I led the way to the dinner table, hoping my walk didn't look as robotic as it felt. I barely had control over my limbs. I felt numb even as I sat and ate and conversed. All I was thinking about was that wire. And the look in those blue eyes—*caught*.

What had he been doing? Well, that was clear enough. He'd been spying. Tampering.

But why? God, it had been bad enough when I'd thought he was in league with Carlos. Carlos would just as soon screw a business partner over if he thought he could get away with it. And he got away with a lot. But to turn the tables and betray Carlos? Shit. Tyler wouldn't just get himself killed. He'd get himself destroyed. Tortured. Maybe his family killed, if he had any left. I remembered he had a mother back when we'd been neighbors, though she hadn't been home much. God help whatever girl he might be seeing. Although right now that might be me.

The specifics didn't matter. Did he think he could make a few extra bucks somehow, maybe skimming off the top? Or was he thinking he could cut Carlos out of the loop entirely? Whatever. He would lose. And then he would die.

And somehow—*still*—I couldn't let that happen.

I had to warn him. I had to stop him. It wouldn't be easy to dissuade him, I knew that much, if he thought the rewards were big. Besides, I'd seen the stubborn glint in his eyes. But I would try. And I would succeed—I had to.

Maybe I could use my feminine wiles. A wry smile traced my lips at that. Such as they were.

Carlos took a large swallow of wine. "The thing about whores is that you don't want to break them. Then they are worthless. You want to keep them hoping, as if one day they might escape."

"Really? Why is that?" Tyler's voice was flat, emotionless. Was this how he'd sound giving orders to a battered, but not yet broken, whore?

"It gives them a little fight." Carlos's eyes had glassed over, as if he were far away. "That's what you want. A little fight."

"Hmm," Tyler said. "I'll have to keep that in mind. I always thought that you'd want an obedient slave."

"Obedience is only worth anything when it's earned. And trust me, I've earned it. Right, Mia?"

Except I knew he didn't want me to answer. I felt Tyler's eyes on me, but I stared down at my plate, pretending not to care that he wanted to learn how to train a slave.

My opportunity came sooner than I was expecting. The phone in question rang from the corner of the room, vibrating on the table. Tyler and I both froze, as if the phone itself could incriminate us. Incriminate *him*, really, although I was now in league with him by keeping silent. Carlos went over and answered it. He turned back to Tyler, and I held my breath.

"Feel free to amuse yourself with her while I take this," Carlos said mildly.

As soon as Carlos stepped outside, Tyler's gaze snapped to mine like a puzzle piece sliding into place. "Are you going to say anything?" he asked, sounding unconcerned and fooling no one.

I didn't even know where to start. "Jesus, Tyler. Who

the fuck do you think you're messing with here? You're going to get yourself killed, do you understand me? *Killed*."

"That's not important," he said. "I asked if you were going to talk."

"And what if I am?" I asked. "Shit, I probably *should* tell him. Then you can get the hell away from here and never come back."

Then the chair wasn't holding me anymore and my back was against the wall. Tyler's body loomed above me.

"This isn't a game," he ground out.

His hands were on my wrists, holding them, squeezing them. I didn't like to be restrained. Maybe I should have been used to it, but hot panic flashed through me. I yanked my arms uselessly. He didn't let go, but he did relax his hold. I took a deep breath, ignoring the racing of my heart.

"What's it going to take?" he asked. "Money? A girl's gotta eat?"

My own words from his lips stung. He thought so little of me, which was somehow more painful than the fact that it was all true. I was the worst sort of whore because I took Carlos's money and then worked to betray him. Because I would convince Tyler he could trust me, and then do anything I could to keep him safe, even if it meant stopping him. Disloyal *puta*.

"Sure," I choked out. "Pay me off."

"How much?" he asked.

"Make an offer." I rolled my body against his.

He sucked in a breath. "Fuck, Mia."

"Fuck, Mia," I mimicked. It was immature, but I didn't care. He already thought the worst of me. He could beat the insolence out of me when he bought me. If Carlos didn't kill us first.

"How much to get you to leave?" he asked. "Permanently. Go far away."

It was my turn to suck in a breath. His disgust of me went deeper than I'd thought. Pain rattled around in my chest like a pin ball before finally dropping down into the pit of my stomach. Men had hated me before him, but at least they'd *wanted* me, even if it was only for sex and to act as the occasional punching bag. Despite the erection poking my stomach, he didn't want me. He wanted to get rid of me.

Who was I kidding? I couldn't blame him. If I could get rid of me, I'd do it in a heartbeat. I stared at the pulse that beat in the hollow of his throat, so steady.

I had no fight left, no hope. "Carlos would find me. He'd kill me."

Tyler must have recognized that I didn't pose a threat to him because he let me go. But he didn't back up. He stood, broad chest to heaving breasts, breath to breath.

"I'd protect you," he said.

My laugh rang out like the rattle of an empty tin cup. "You and what army?"

"Not the army," he said pointedly.

My eyes snapped to his. And the final chink fell, like a deadbolt locking into place. Witness protection…the Holy Grail that had been dangled in front of me by another man just recently. That man had been with the FBI, and I realized that Tyler was one of them, undercover. Of course. A laugh burbled to the surface. Inappropriate, this entire situation was inappropriate. "You're faking it, aren't you? You're the fucking cops."

He frowned and glanced around, adorably peeved.

I couldn't believe I hadn't thought of it myself. The golden boy of the neighborhood, the soldier, Mr. Perfect. He could never have been a bad guy, the lighting was all wrong.

I thought of Zachary, Carlos's nephew and my contact in the FBI. Dark hair, a grim mouth, and tortured eyes. That was a man who belonged in the underworld. Only an irrepressible sense of honor had kept him on the straight and narrow despite his familial ties.

They couldn't have been more opposite, Zachary and Tyler. One man's redemption, the other a fallen angel. But it turned out they worked together, fought together. I was just a pawn on the board.

"Know a guy named Zachary?" I asked.

He stiffened. "Why?"

"He's my contact," I whispered, giving myself away, trusting him once again.

His eyes narrowed. I could see when he got it, when he understood that I was with the FBI as well. "I knew Zachary had an informant, but…" He trailed off, looking almost disappointed. Well, I could guess why. He couldn't get rid of me as long as I was an informant, as long as I supplied him and Zachary with information.

"What was all that shit about buying me then?" I demanded.

He looked away and then back at me, guiltily. "I was just trying to get him out of the room."

It seemed like a stretch. He wanted to see the phone, so he goaded Carlos into dragging me off to his cave like a Neanderthal. Well, I was used to getting played. The disappointment stabbed a little deeper than I expected. As much as his offer to buy me from Carlos had made him a dick, I'd liked the interest he'd taken in me. It felt good to be wanted. Now I knew I was just a feint, a slight of hand.

Look over there, fuck that girl, while I take what I need.

Well, I told myself, be grateful that he's really a good guy. It had eaten me up to think I'd been wrong about him. Or that the world had so hardened him that he'd turned criminal. But his halo was safely shiny, blinding beside the worn-down horns of a whore.

He put his hand on mine, grounding me. "Can I trust you?"

Could he trust me? Yes, to the ends of the earth. I would die for him. That part wasn't a huge sacrifice, considering, but more than that, I would kill for him. Anything he wanted, though it was probably for the best that he didn't know that.

"Yes," I said.

"Good," he said, though the air around us stank with doubt and suspicion. "We can meet up later. Just lay low."

He pulled his hand back as Carlos came into the room, walking away like he didn't know me, like he didn't care.

CHAPTER FOUR

THE AIR IN the shadowed corridor vibrated with a presence just before Leo grabbed me and slammed me against a wall in an alcove. My body was a fluid thing, accustomed to moving with the flow, bending but not breaking. I took the hit without a sound.

"What's with the new guy?" he growled.

Leo would see Tyler as competition. Hell, he *was* Leo's competition.

Where I was Carlos's cock-sucking whore, Leo was his right-hand man. I'd heard they were distant cousins or something, which was a big plus for a guy like Carlos. I was shocked he'd brought in someone on the outside for something so important. He must be nervous. Or maybe Leo was on the outs, but if that were the case, he shouldn't even be breathing.

"I don't know. It's some big deal they have going down."

Leo shook me, banging my head against the wall. It was a testament to how upset he was, because he usually tried not to hurt me, except for the times Carlos wanted him to hurt me.

"Stop dicking around," he said. "You know about

the girls. And you know that's what Martinez is here for. I want to know what happened last night."

"What do you think happened? I was supposed to 'entertain' the new guy. You think they consult with me on business matters?"

"You have ears."

I sighed. "Look, I want the new guy gone as much as you. But I don't have a say either."

"Did he hurt you?" Leo looked down at my body, as if he could see my injuries through my clothes. It wasn't like when Tyler had asked me that, though, with a mix of horror and hesitation. Leo was downright curious.

He had a sadistic nature just like Carlos. The difference was that he also had a conscience. So he tried to hide his sadism, to repress it, and maybe even would have been successful if he hadn't hooked up with a guy like Carlos. Carlos made use of Leo's propensity for giving pain, whether it was to torture information out of an enemy or punish a slut for his amusement.

"Not more than usual."

"Okay." Leo released me. I was always being slammed up against walls, forever having to redeem myself to men. And maybe I wouldn't have minded so much if they gave a shit about me in the end.

I pushed him off me. He was a big guy, though, very strong. When he stumbled back, it was all for show. Sometimes he let me throw a little tantrum, and I did, stalking off in a huff.

When I reached my room, I shut the door and stuck

the thick wad of paper under the door as a wedge to keep it shut. Then I pulled out the disposable cell phone from the fake bottom of my dresser drawer. It was time to check-in with my contact.

"Do you have any news?" Zachary's voice was scratchy on the satellite phone, but anything local could be traced. Carlos may have been old school, but Zachary didn't take any chances. The Russians would have access to all kinds of technology, he said.

"Yeah," I said. "I met your guy on the inside."

His whistle crackled through the static. "You made him?"

Yes, I'd realized Tyler was a cop. "Guy's the worst kind," I groused. "Total do-gooder."

"And Carlos?"

"He's got no idea. Thinks he's grooming the guy to be the next him."

Zachary chuckled. I didn't think every informant got the friendly treatment, but I wasn't just any informant. I'd saved Zachary's life and his girlfriend's when Carlos had tried to blow them up six months ago. That was how we'd met, them fighting for their lives, me giving an assist. He'd made contact shortly after that. He rejoined the investigation and asked me to help.

I knew Zachary's superiors gave him shit about trusting my intel, but he'd always displayed complete faith in me. His superiors were right, though. I wasn't trustworthy, as evidenced by the fact that I was betraying Carlos at all. Never trust a traitor. Still, a bond forms when you've taken a man's life in your hands, like a spider's thread, thin but strong.

I didn't want to let Zachary down. I didn't want to let those girls in the shipment down. And maybe, impossibly, I wanted Tyler to be proud of me. What a sap.

"He got a call from them yesterday. They're moving up their timetable. They're talking in the next *week*, not months."

"Are you sure?" Zachary asked sharply.

"I'm sure," I said wryly, thinking of how Carlos's cock had wilted, just a little, in my mouth when the guy on the other end of the line had started berating him. Men had no idea how much they gave away in their quest for control.

"They wanted to talk about security, but I guess you already know about that." Seeing as the head of Carlos's security was actually an undercover agent.

"Give me the run-down anyway."

"They just said they need more. More security—more men, more guns."

"And my guy, he trusts him?"

I thought about that. Carlos wasn't the alpha dog—he was the rabid one. If anyone even looked at him sideways, he felt the need to attack, to display his dominance, and then shit on the person just for good measure.

Tyler challenged him, I could see that. With his obvious physical competence at combat, something illustrated not only by the toned muscles that filled out his body, but also by the fact that he was head of security and clearly knew his way around a weapons rack, Carlos would be feeling the urge to fight.

But Carlos also acted with a certain camaraderie with Tyler, one I'd never seen him display for his other underlings. It was almost like he saw Tyler as his equal. That fact might mean Tyler's downfall in the end, but for now it kept him in a position of favored pupil. Besides the fact that there was a lot of money riding on this deal, millions of dollars, and he needed Tyler.

"I think he's okay," I finally said. "Carlos seems to respect him."

"Good," Zachary said. "And you? Does he suspect anything?"

I snorted. "Do you think I'd be breathing if he did?"

"Okay. Be careful."

The static ended abruptly, signaling the end of the call.

Be careful. Oh, yes, I had a care or two. Things to take care of before I died, but none of it would change the ending. I was like those cartoon characters that ran and ran and looked down, only to find themselves already off a cliff. I'd left solid ground the second I'd supplied Zachary with information. It was only a matter of time before I fell.

In my closet, one of the few rooms free of cameras, I stowed the phone under the fake bottom of my lingerie drawer. Then I curled up on the cozy bed and read a book. It passed the time anyway, and Carlos liked to find me that way. It made him chuckle that I would read a book, that I had a thought in my head when all I was good for was a cock in the mouth. He appreciated irony, one of the few things we had in common.

But it wasn't Carlos who found me that way.

Tyler stormed in, his face set in sharp slashes of fury. Instinctively, I pulled my knees under me, ready to flee, and put my hands up in defense. He didn't attack me though, at least not in the way I expected. His hands knocked mine aside and then his lips met mine. It wasn't a kiss, it was an accusation.

My mind spun like a top, dizzy. My body had no such confusion, melting into his angry embrace, wetting the thin line of my thong.

He flipped me over, and I went down, face first. The silk sheets cooled my cheek, chilling the ardor I barely knew existed. Then his mouth was against my ear, whispering.

"Was it you?" he asked. "Did you tell him after all, hmm?"

Still sluggish from the surprise or maybe the arousal, I said, "I don't know what you're talking about."

"Don't you? Someone told him about a traitor. He's gone nuts."

I sucked in a breath. The kiss, what I'd taken to be seduction, had merely been for the cameras that weren't even in this room, to distract from the fact that he wanted to have a conversation. Though conversation was too nice a word for the accusations he flung.

"I didn't say anything," I hissed. "Why would I risk him suspecting me?"

"I don't know. Maybe you're not an informant at all. Maybe you're just feeding me what he wants me to think."

Anger washed over me, drowning out the hurt. I shook him off. He allowed me to turn over, but his body kept me trapped against the bed. It was more intimate this way, more sexual. The sky blue of his eyes shocked me, so close. I saw them plenty in my dreams, but always from afar. Even my subconscious knew it was hopeless.

"I thought you trusted me," came out on an exhale. *Damn.* I clamped my mouth shut, hadn't meant to say that.

"I'd be an idiot to trust you," he replied.

I took the sting as my due. Tyler was a lot of things, but never an idiot. It always came back to this. The ceiling swam above me, as if it were the surface of the ocean and I lay on the sandy floor. This must be why it shocked me to look him in the eye, I realized. There was too much truth there, too much knowledge. It was like looking into the sun—painful. *Just look down.*

"I don't know how I can convince you," I said. "I'm telling the truth."

"Then prove it," he said into my neck, still playing at the farce of a make-out session. "He's got an idea that someone's dirty…someone else who's undercover. We're in trouble."

"And what should I do—sacrifice myself?" I raised my eyebrow, though I wasn't entirely sure he wouldn't ask it of me.

"He's going to go find him now, and it won't go well. It would blow the whole thing, not to mention mean a death sentence for that guy. I need time to get them out. A distraction."

Ah, so I was to be the sacrifice after all. Not a virgin, not anywhere close, but a sacrificial whore.

"Okay," I said, as if it didn't matter, as if it didn't hurt when he sent me into harm's way. It was different with Zachary. With him it was all business and maybe a little camaraderie, but he never took me for granted.

Tyler seemed to think nothing of using me to achieve his ends. His goals were noble, saving those women, but what about me? People who said the end justified the means were never the ones suffering the means. I wasn't really complaining about my lot in life. No, I'd accepted my whoredom years ago. What shook me was that Tyler accepted it so easily as well.

"Can you do it?" he asked.

"I said yes already," I snapped. He didn't just think I was a whore, he thought I was a bad one. I led the way downstairs. We found Carlos outside. Tyler went first, conversing with Carlos in front of a black SUV. I took a minute to collect myself, and then joined them.

"I'll see for myself," Carlos said.

"All right," Tyler said. "Go on, then. I'll see you on the sensor from here."

He sounded so wholly unconcerned that I would never have known he was worried about it. But if he betrayed any sign that he wanted Carlos to stay, it would be a dead giveaway.

"Go inside," Carlos snapped when he saw me.

"Baby," I purred, draping my arms around his neck. "I miss you. Come spend time with me. I'll make you feel so good."

He twisted my wrist, flipping my body to the ground in a graceless heap. I caught a glimpse of shocked blue eyes and realized Tyler hadn't fully understood the violence Carlos directed at me. Even though he worked in the darkness, his mind was filled with light. Tyler couldn't imagine inflicting that kind of violence on someone, because he never, ever would. And the one time we had been together, he hadn't seen my scars.

Just as quickly he masked his shock. It wasn't a surprise because he was good at his job. That's why we were here after all, him acting nonchalant and me getting my ass beat. And it was working, as Carlos leaned over me, spitting in my face with his lecture about interrupting my betters.

"You sniveling little whore," he raged. "Like I don't give you everything. A place to stay, food to eat, fancy clothes, and how do you repay me? By getting in my way, demanding more. Greedy *puta*."

I cowered—that part came naturally. And if I wanted to, I could simper, ingratiate myself to him in order to cool his wrath. But that wouldn't serve Tyler's purpose.

If Carlos forgot about me, he'd be right back to blowing the sting operation along with Tyler's cover.

Already cringing for the blow, I mouthed off. "It's only because you never pay attention to me. I don't see what's the big deal."

The blow came, harder than I expected. It was always harder than I expected, no matter how many times I'd been hit. Sex was routine, but muscle memory refused to let me accustom to beatings. As if my own body was working with Carlos, I felt every hit, every cut, like it was my first.

My face pressed against the grass, incongruously smelling like a fresh spring day and the tang of blood. Carlos yanked up my skirt and spanked me. These weren't the playful, kinky spanks of a lover, but the beating of a man on a woman. His arm wielded as a club, not stinging, bruising.

I kept my grunts as soft as possible, not wanting to arouse anymore of Carlos's ire, not wanting to show Tyler how badly it hurt. He would feel bad if he knew. Even though it was his fault, I didn't want him to take the blame.

Tears leaked from my eyes, mixing with the dirt under my face, drawing camouflage on my face. I tried not to imagine how horrible I must look when Carlos yanked me back to stand up.

"Jesus," Carlos said. "Look what you did. I have work to do and now I'm busy dealing with a fucking brat." He shook me as if for an answer, but there wasn't a question.

"Martinez, go check on the safehouse," Carlos barked to Tyler.

A thick pause followed. What was he waiting for? This was exactly what Tyler needed, ample opportunity for his men to finish whatever operation they were doing and to get out, safe and undetected.

I flicked my eyes up to find Tyler staring, not at me or even Carlos, but at some point directly in front of me. His eyes burned with intensity, but what it meant, I didn't know. Anger maybe, for a job well done. He reminded me of myself in that moment, unable to look upon the object of his disappointment. That would be me, I thought sickly, the elephant in the room, the object of shame.

"Well?" Carlos asked, his silken voice a warning.

"I'm going." Tyler yanked open the door to the SUV so hard it rocked on its axle. With one foot inside, he paused as if debating with himself. Without turning, he said, "It shouldn't take too long. Maybe half an hour. Then I'll be back and we can go over the new security procedures."

He spoke to Carlos, but the message was for me, telling me that he would be back to relieve me soon. Tyler had no idea how much damage could be inflicted in even ten minutes when Carlos was enraged. And I'd *never* been quite so brazen in my disobedience.

CHAPTER FIVE

"**D**ID YOU THINK you could interrupt me?"

Thump. The leather belt smacked me between the shoulders. The first blows were always the hardest to take. At least, that's what I thought until we got to the ones that came after. It was always a shock, every blow, as if my mind had dimmed the memory of every pain before.

"Do you think I care what you want? What you think?"

Thwack. The force of the impact jolted my body like the flop of a limp doll on concrete. The pain followed in a wave of aftershocks, radiating from my back out to my fingertips. I couldn't breathe, couldn't think, couldn't even see anything. A haze of red blanketed my vision, heightening the pain.

"You are *nothing* to me. Just a whore, and a stupid one at that."

Crack. The belt bit into my back, coiling around my ribs to lick the underside of my breast. A short scream escaped me, abruptly cut off with the impact of the next blow. It rang in the air though—the searing pain, my agony—as he beat me.

He was hurting me because I'd annoyed him, but the truth of the matter was that I'd only done it for Tyler. I'd betrayed Carlos, and so I deserved the punishment. I deserved worse than this, though as my body lit on fire from the outside in, I couldn't imagine anything more painful.

What could hell have to offer me that could compete with this? Maybe God was just expedient that way, getting in some of my licks while I still lived. Or maybe I'd already died, and I would be stuck in this hell for eternity. That was the scariest thought of all. The only thing that made this bearable was knowing that one day I would be free of it. Even hell had to be better than this.

I heard the slice come through the air, just an innocuous whistle, before the single tail whip flayed my skin. The screams rang out from my throat, wholly detached from my mind. I couldn't control them anymore than I could control the whip. My skin seared where it split open. As the pain tore through my body, sweat broke out, dripping into the open wounds, burning me. Even my own body betrayed me, causing more pain, showing more weakness.

They went on and on, each flail of the whip cutting me open, tearing me apart until I was sure I'd never get put back together again. The pain crashed over me in never-ending waves, pulling me under only to thrust me back up to the awareness again.

Pain continued to reverberate through my back as if he'd never stopped, but he was in front of me, waving his dick in my face. Slapping me, wetting me with the pre-cum at the tip. A jerk of my hair opened my mouth, and then it was filled with cock. Years of training, a lifetime of it, kicked in and I laved the underside with my tongue, relaxed my throat to allow him in deep.

Bite him. The thought occurred to me, not for the first time, as he fucked my face harshly. I'd die for the transgression, an ugly, painful death with no dignity. Fear and an unshakeable desire for survival had kept me from doing it all this time, but now it wasn't just my own hide, broken and scarred as it was, on the line. There were those nameless, faceless girls who still had hope for a life.

And there was Tyler. He was counting on me to help him. He'd asked me to distract Carlos. This was the only way I could. So I sucked him and let my face be raped mercilessly. Every rough thrust was like a coin slipped into the game for one more round—he'd be distracted that much longer. Tyler would be that much safer. The piercing pain of Carlos's dick popping into my throat, the acute cramp in my neck from craning upward, the hands tight in my hair were the ride itself, a fun-house torture chamber.

He came with a soft grunt, music to my ears. Salty liquid splashed into the back of my throat. I swallowed it down, knowing that a single drop lost would only mean more pain. The only people who said that you attracted more bees with honey had never been whipped.

Only once I had balked at swallowing. My childhood

training had taught me a lot of things about being a woman, but that particular lesson had been missing. I'd been surprised at the gush of ejaculate. I'd gagged and coughed it out. My punishment that night had been to swallow from every man Carlos had working for him. I learned that lesson well.

A soft beep pierced the curtain my mind had constructed to protect me from reality, the innocuous bleep of the cell phone incongruous to the noxious blend of blood and rage that hung in the air.

"Tyler. You back yet?" Carlos snapped. "All right. I'll be up in a minute."

The phone clapped shut and his boots stomped away from me. Without a word, he left, shutting the door and closing me in darkness. I hung my head and slipped away.

My jaw felt like it had turned to stone, clenched shut. Only the low moan emanating from it—from me—told me I was alive. I didn't want to move. Even in the cocoon of sleep I knew that as soon as I became conscious, as soon as I moved a muscle, the pain would retaliate. A jealous mistress, pain would be too eager to make up for the time lost to dreams.

But a body keeps on living. I'd learned that lesson early on. Would he come back? Was my punishment over? *God, let it be over.*

I wasn't in the basement. The smell of blood and

leather wasn't here. I figured Carlos had sent Leo down to free me, to put me back in my room. I just hoped he hadn't given Leo permission to use me first, like he sometimes did.

My eyes flickered open, shooting warning shocks of pain through me and signaling the nausea to begin. I was coming back to life, despite myself.

"Shhh. I've got you." I heard Tyler's soothing over a mournful wail. It was coming from me.

His hand stroked down my face in a calming caress, but its path was carefully picked, as if to avoid the bruises there like brambles in a thicket. I'd never wanted him to see me like this.

I tried to speak again. A croaked sound emerged.

"Shh, just rest. You're okay."

He sounded so sure, but I had to know. "Where is he?"

"He's not here, don't worry." But the reassurance came on a razor's edge.

I tossed restlessly in the bed, ferreting out every ache, every bruise.

"Where is he?" I whispered again.

"He's out meeting with the suppliers. Trying to calm them down." Tyler paused. "We got the guy out. You did it." His voice cracked at the last. "God," he said, more a sob than a word. "I thought—I never imagined he would do *this*. Why, Mia? Why do you stay?"

"Where would I go?" It was a rhetorical question, a flippant answer, but it was the closest thing to the truth.

Blinking, I recognized the open ceiling of the warehouse I called home, the exposed rafters and pipes blanketed with dust like moss on a tree. The sheets weren't slippery like Carlos's silk or coarse like the threadbare sheets in my own bed. These were soft, and like Goldilocks, I found them just right. I guessed we were in Tyler's room in the compound, though how he'd gotten me out of the basement I had no idea.

"But—*fuck*, Mia. I thought maybe he'd fuck you. Maybe even slap you, if I let myself think about it. But not *this*. Your back…" His eyes held the horror of what had been done to me, they begged to understand, so I searched for something more concrete.

I struggled with that, understanding it all myself. "Carlos isn't all bad," I finally said.

Tyler's eyes flitted down to my bruises and then back to my face in a tacit denial.

I sighed. "He took me in when I was starving, when I didn't have anywhere else to go."

"When was this?" Tyler asked tightly.

I'd have to tell him my story, I realized. I did owe him that. Or maybe that was just an excuse for wanting to unload on someone. I could share my story as long as I left out certain details about my father. I saw the guilt that pricked him from what had happened to me today and knew, instinctively, that it would eat him up to know the full situation in which he'd left me back then. I knew that he hadn't owed me anything, couldn't have known, but he wouldn't see it that way.

"My father was…well, he got drunk a lot. And when he got drunk, he got violent." I ignored the sharp intake of Tyler's breath. I didn't think my father's rages could have been totally unknown to Tyler, living so closely to me as he had, but he hadn't realized the extent. And he never would, not if I could help it.

I could see him forming the questions already. *How soon did the violence start? Was I there when you were getting hurt?* He wouldn't like the answers to them, not if I was honest, so I moved on quickly.

"I got fed up and ran away," I said. "I lived on the streets, but I was starving. Starving and broke. I don't think I had more than a few days left in me when Carlos found me in an alley."

I gave Tyler a wry smile. "He was popping some guy for who knows what. I was behind some boxes, but I must have made a sound. Carlos pulled me out and I thought for sure he'd kill me. But instead he took me home. He cleaned me up, fed me, took care of me all this time."

Tyler's jaw was clenched hard, with only a vein popping in his temple and the faint flare of his nostrils for movement. His eyes turned on me, a revelation of shared pain. "He took advantage of you."

I laughed softly. "There wasn't anything to take advantage of, just skin and bones. He had to nurse me back to health. And then, yes, he did expect repayment, but it was only fair." I'd been paying for my food and clothes and a roof over my head with my body since I was young. That wasn't going to change in my lifetime. It was my one constant.

Tyler stood up and walked away from me, only the stiff correctness of his posture betraying his upset. If he had only been a little agitated, only a tiny bit unnerved, it would have been okay. But he was beyond that, beyond bothered and well into rage. I couldn't help but be scared so soon after my recent encounter with Carlos's fury.

He must have seen my reaction, a small withdrawal, because he turned stricken.

I softened at that. "It's okay. It's been okay. Not so bad. But a few months ago…there was this girl. I mean, I'm not the only girl to have ever been here, but this one was different. Carlos really gave her a hard time, more than usual, and I could tell—" I wasn't sure how to explain the wounded look in her eyes, the one I recognized in the mirror. "—I could tell she'd had it rough. It was bad enough, but when he tried to kill her, I couldn't let it happen."

I shrugged. "So I saved her. Her and Zachary. Then Zachary told me about the trafficking and recruited me as an informant. And…well, at least I can do some good here."

Tyler hung his head. "Fuck, Mia. I know you said you weren't his girlfriend, but I thought you were. And I guess you are, in a way, but it wasn't…I never thought he'd do this to you. I thought you were just like any other girlfriend of a criminal, that you either didn't care about what he did or you liked the rewards too much to bother with it."

"Hey," I said with a hand on his arm. "That's pretty much true. For a long time I didn't care about the bad stuff he did."

"You were a kid!" he burst out.

I cringed at his volume, his words.

"I'm sorry," he said, his voice as hoarse as if he'd been shouting for hours instead of minutes. "I'm sorry. I just can't…I can't quite get a handle on it. It'll take me some time."

He looked up at me, earnestness glistening in his eyes, never looking more like the young golden boy than right now. "I'm just ashamed that I didn't know you did this out of desperation. I knew it wasn't good for you here, but I thought that you chose to be here."

"I did."

But we both knew what would happen to me if I left. I'd known for a long time that the only way out of Carlos's cold embrace was six feet under. And after seeing the results of Carlos's punishment, it seemed Tyler understood as well. But just because death was unsavory didn't make it any less of a choice, and one day soon, I'd give in to it. Just not today.

"I want you to leave."

I rolled my eyes. "Do you say that to all the ladies? Because I can't imagine that gets you a lot of play."

"I'm serious," he insisted. "It's like I told you before. You can go into Witness Protection. I can keep you safe."

He might as well have been offering to ship me to a colony on Mars for all that a safe life meant anything real to me.

"And what's going to happen to those girls?" I reminded him. "Carlos was already freaked about a traitor. If I wind up missing, he's going to know something was up. And he'll probably suspect I had help getting away, too. The whole operation will be blown. Those girls will end up sold somewhere else entirely and you'll never find them."

Tyler said nothing, knew I was right.

"So I'll stay," I said quietly. There was a solemnity, a finality, to the statement that I felt in my bones. This would be the last thing I did with Carlos. However it ended, with success or failure, it *would* end. And then maybe I'd find peace, even if it was in a pine box.

"I'll protect you," Tyler swore vehemently.

I smiled, tinged with sadness. "You can't even trust me. How can you protect me?"

"I will," he insisted. "And I trust you now. I'm sorry, so sorry. And I want to make that up to you, too, but for now I hope you'll settle for protection and trust."

"Okay," I agreed, with a detached indulgence.

"You'll be fine," he said, though who he was trying to convince, I didn't know. "And when this is all over, I'll set you up somewhere safe. You'll start a new life, away from all this."

I told him okay to that, too. There was time enough for the truth later.

CHAPTER SIX

I STUDIED TYLER'S unfathomable expression through the mirror as I applied foundation to my bruises. I worked at my vanity, fixing myself, hiding. He lounged in the corner chair, watching me.

The casual pose might have fooled a woman with less experience in reading a man's body language. But the wide flung arms and spread thighs were taut like a panther ready to pounce. His eyes held an intensity I'd learned to be wary of many men ago.

He'd insisted on walking me back to my room and making sure I was settled—and stable—before getting back to work. Apparently that included voyeurism of my cosmetic routine. Not that his gaze was sexual. It was predatory.

After the base and foundation, I laid on the loose powder. A good make-up job was a matter of thin layers, well-blended, as opposed to thick smudges. I could probably have an alternate career as a make-up artist, assuming I lived long enough to stop being a whore. Assuming I were normal enough not to be a whore. Not that respectable places would hire me. I was already dead on paper, having disappeared from school at sixteen and never having filed any official paperwork or taxes since then. The system probably counted me rotting in an alley years ago. Sometimes I wondered if that wouldn't have been the better fate.

Maybe I could work in the underground as a make-up artist to the battered wives of the rich and famous. Blotting away bruises and covering up cuts was an art form, one I'd had plenty of opportunity to perfect. The messiest to fix were open wounds, where the skin gaped open, exposing bloody tissue or worse. Those were best left alone and explained away as an accident of some sort. Otherwise I was looking at putty or air-brushing, which got time consuming and expensive.

Not that it was my dime. As long as Carlos made the bruises, Carlos paid for them to be covered up. Besides, he was the one who insisted I go out looking like gold as soon as I could drag myself out of the pool of blood and other liquids. I would have preferred to curl up in my bed, the one that Tyler had been eyeing ever since he'd followed me into my room.

My bedroom was smaller than Carlos's bedroom, even smaller than Tyler's. Barely a bedroom at all, it fit my twin-size bed, a vanity, and a beat-up dresser for my clothes. Carlos used the tiny room as a reminder of my status, as if I actually needed one considering what I did. I never entertained men here so I didn't need a big bed. I actually preferred it this way, to have a space I could keep to myself, no matter how small. Carlos would probably take it away if he realized that.

Tyler had invaded it today. I felt his presence, his intrusion, like a sharp pebble in my shoe.

"Does this get you hot?" I asked just to rile him up.

He drummed his fingers on his thighs, not taking the bait.

"I know you're here for a reason. Just spit it out. Need me to take a few more licks? Want a blow job?"

That got him. He stiffened in his seat and glowered. His heart wasn't in it though. Poor man was still freaked out over my injuries. He didn't realize that I'd long ago become inured to them. The pain could touch my skin, but no deeper. And if that was because there wasn't anything left inside, all the better.

With a last brush of powder, I turned and approached Tyler, using my best sexy walk.

"You're so tense," I cooed, not missing a beat at noticing a bulge rise from his pants. "I can kiss it better."

"Stop it," he snapped. "I know this isn't you."

I laughed. "If that's what you think, then you don't know me at all."

He shook his head, nostrils flaring. "You were forced into this. Men abused you. They hurt you. *I* hurt you."

Of course. His mind didn't want to think of sweet little Mia from next door as a dirty skank. So he was excusing it away. But I didn't like it. For reasons I couldn't begin to explain, I wanted him to see me. To know me, even if that knowledge disgusted him.

"Don't pity me," I said sharply. Then softer, "I wasn't forced, baby. Maybe a few times, but they knew what I was good for."

A small choked sound came out of him, but I pushed on.

"Most of the time...I chose to do it. I used to be cheap. Just to hear him tell me I was a good girl, that was the price of a blow job. Later I got a little more expensive, a few bucks so I could go get food for dinner or buy clothes that fit me when I grew out of my old ones. But Carlos, he turned me into what I am today. Fancy clothes, fancy make-up, fancy dates when he takes me out. A girl like me couldn't ask for better."

Sometime during my little speech I'd gotten angry. I was yelling, ranting, incensed that he could think good of me when there wasn't any good to be found. "So if you've gotten it in your head that my father tied me down or that Carlos put a gun to my head to get me in here, you're all wrong. Okay? You're wrong."

The vision of Tyler swam before my eyes like one of those swirly paintings, beautiful and morbid. I felt his breath in my hair, shushing me, telling me to stop, that it would be okay, and his hands on my arms, pulling me close, burning the cuts there. He probably didn't remember I was bruised there too, not just my back, but I didn't want him to stop. Whatever touch he had to offer me, I would take. Whatever pain he would give me, I deserved.

I choked out a sob against his chest, so warm, so solid.

"Mia," he said. "Mia."

Whatever he meant by that, it didn't matter. He was here. I had to be grateful for that.

Don't leave, I wanted to beg. *Don't ever leave.* But begging never worked. My cheeks dampened with impotent tears, as I mourned the loss of the man, of his comfort, before he'd even left.

"Shhh," he said. "I'm going to fix this. I don't know how yet, but I am."

A watery laugh trickled out of me. I thought of that nursery rhyme, the one about Humpty Dumpty. *All the king's horses and all the king's men couldn't put Humpty together again.*

"You can't fix me," I whispered, the tears catching on my lips. "No one can."

"No," he said fiercely. "This is my fault. I should have known. I think…maybe I did know, but I was too fucking stupid to know what to do about it. If I would have done something back then, got you out of there…"

The image rose up in my mind, like a specter from the grave. Me, without shame. Without fear. It was a laughable thought, but somehow…somehow hopeful. Somehow heartbreaking.

"God, don't do this," I told him. "Don't make me think impossible things."

"Listen. Let's just get through this. We'll get through this thing with Carlos together, you and me. And when it's all over, we'll work on fixing this together. I don't know exactly how it will go. A lot of that will depend on you and what you want to do. But sure as hell you're not going to be anyone's whore, not ever again."

He sounded so sure, so confident. So much the fresh-faced young man about to set off on his adventure. Like maybe he'd sit down next to me on an old, dirty tire and say, "It can't be as bad as all that." Just as optimistic, just as wrong.

I didn't want to tell him that I probably wouldn't survive *this*, this thing we were doing with Carlos. I could feel myself weakening after each session with him. Each time it took me a little longer to recover, more time to heal. And Carlos was getting more brutal, not less, even though I was mostly obedient.

I didn't want to tell him that even if by some miracle I made it out of this alive, that I had nothing and nowhere to go. And if Tyler ended up helping me in exchange for sex, I had no doubt that I would be *his* prostitute. He might be a gentler master, but that didn't make me any less a whore.

I didn't want to say any of that because it would ruin this moment, this moment where Tyler acted like he cared about me. Hell, in this moment, he probably did care about me. So I just leaned into him, letting my make-up smudge, letting my aches and bruises cry out for respite, because this feeling was worth a million lashes.

When my tears dried, I looked up at him. Some of the fierceness in his expression was now explained away. He felt some responsibility for what happened to me. But he wasn't my knight in shining armor, no matter how much I might have wished him to be.

"Tell me what you need me to do," I said.

His mouth firmed in refusal, which told me that he did, in fact, have something he needed me to do.

"Come on," I cajoled, with a soft rock of my breasts into his chest. It was almost instinctual at this point, not something mapped out or planned, using my body to get on a guy's good side. Even broken and battered, it worked.

"I don't want you to do this." But despite his words, his tone held resignation. "We can get the girls to safety once we're inside the safe house. The problem is there's a master key for the alarm system that is only released by Carlos's fingerprint."

I watched him, waiting.

"He won't exactly be cooperative with us," Tyler continued. "In fact, if all goes according to plan, he won't even be there when we're extracting the women. So there's this—" He held up a small rectangular box, black plastic with a shiny metal strip on one side. "That has the capability to record not only the form of the fingerprint, but also the heat patterns. Using this we'll be able to replicate it and unlock the system without his presence. You need to press his right thumbprint to the metal surface for five seconds. Without him noticing."

"Yeah." An incredulous laugh escaped me. No blow job was good enough for Carlos to miss me taking his fingerprint with a device. I wondered if Tyler saw the irony, that he was using my body for his own purposes. I almost hoped he didn't, since at least that way it would be accidental.

Tyler paused as if biting his tongue.

"There's more," I said.

"You'll need to get out. There are a few different ways this might play out, but no matter what he'll suspect you had something to do with it."

I scoffed. "Carlos thinks of me like a dog. Animals can't be informants."

He ignored me. "They'll set you up with a new name, a new life, the whole bit. All you have to do is cut out when Carlos leaves for the drop. Just get the hell out of here and drive to the station. Zachary will be waiting for you."

That wasn't the plan at all. The plan was to free the girls and then let Carlos do his worst. I had no doubts that it would be painful, nor did I have any doubts about how it would end. With the sweet release of death. I couldn't tell Tyler that. He wouldn't understand.

"Okay," I said. "Get his fingerprint. Get out when shit goes down. No problem."

He gave me a lopsided smile, heartbreaking with its hopefulness. "Just two more days, and then it will all be over."

An answering smile, more pathetic than anything, flickered on my face. Because I was desperate for the same thing, just not in the way Tyler was. The day I stopped being a whore was the day I died. And I really needed to dissuade him of the notion that everything would end with sunshine and roses. It would only make the inevitable let-down harder. So I used my best whore's smile. The plastic-looking one. "Really? So you and your men are going to carry me off into the sunset, with not a single thank-you blowjob in sight?"

His smile died a quick death.

I was a little too exposed, a little too raw, but I couldn't stop myself, couldn't be strong anymore. "Or, wait, will I even see you again once I meet up with Zachary? Or are you going to be too busy with the operation to even say goodbye?"

"God, Mia. Give me a little credit."

"I'm sorry," I said, somehow immediately contrite. It was a practiced thing, apologies, demurring to a man, but in this case I meant it. He'd given me no indication not to trust him, not counting the bulge in his pants whenever he looked at me.

"No, I'm sorry," he said tightly. "I don't deserve any credit. Let's just get this over with."

He stalked from the room, all angry male pride. I'd have been lying if I said I didn't look at his ass as he went. I didn't lust after men's bodies. They'd brought me way too much pain to ever make me *want* them, to desire them. But I could appreciate Tyler's body in a remote kind of way. Like if I had to lie with a man—and women, we did have to—his wouldn't be such a bad one to do it with. If a body had to hurt me, I wouldn't mind as much if it were his.

Only it seemed he didn't want me. Not back then and not now. But it didn't matter, because no matter what happened with those girls, no matter what happened with Tyler, I wasn't getting out of this alive.

CHAPTER SEVEN

CARLOS WAS SURPRISED to see me in his study bright and early. Most times, if I got a beating, I spent the next few days making myself scarce, slinking around like a kicked stray dog. It helped to make sure my wounds were healed before he got another go at me. And the extra time meant he could work out whatever anger was left on other people.

But there I was, dressed in my sluttiest clothes, and that was saying something. A bikini probably would have been more conservative, but Carlos would recognize it for what it was: an apology. Groveling.

Appreciation filled his gaze as he studied me. Not appreciation for my curves, which he'd seen clothed and naked and every which way, but for the blush of shame tinting my skin. It was a long walk from my small room to his study, and I'd passed more than a few suggestive leers and pinching fingers on the way.

He didn't open his arms to me or pat his knee. He didn't even open his fly to make me suck his cock. Never a good sign.

"What do you want?" he asked with the indulgent amusement of a man sure in his victory.

"I'm sorry I bothered you yesterday. I want to make it up to you. Please, Carlos." I didn't have to make my voice sultry, it was already hoarse from screaming. I wasn't a good enough actor to feign the fearful tremor or submissive posture, but I didn't have to be.

This small action, approaching Carlos this way, was about the ballsiest thing I'd ever done. Maybe no one else would see it that way, but I didn't think too many other people had an appreciation for just how badly this could go for me. It was like approaching a rabid dog. All the caution in the world wouldn't protect you if you stuck your hand in its mouth.

"You want to make it up to me?" he asked.

"Yes, Carlos."

"You want to be my whore?"

"Yes, Carlos."

"You want to be my pet?"

A lump caught in my throat.

I'd told Tyler that Carlos thought of me as a dog. His pet. Tyler had thought it was an analogy, a play on words. He'd been wrong.

About six months ago, I'd gotten the idea to leave. Well, I'd had it sooner than that, but I finally decided to act on it. I'd looked up a shelter and packed a few things. I made it a few blocks over before Leo caught up to me. Carlos had him beat the shit out of me, again and again, but that was the punishment phase. The first phase.

Then there was atonement.

I had to get myself out of the doghouse, figuratively

and literally. He made me his puppy, his bitch. I crawled around on the hard concrete, only allowed to bark or whimper. At least he put a dog bed on the cold floor for me.

I thought I'd ingratiated myself to Carlos within the first couple of days, but he kept me at it for almost a week just because it amused him so much. The worst part of it, to me, was that on the floor, anyone was allowed to touch me. Anyone could fuck me. Hurt me.

Strange men, rough men, regularly came through the warehouse headquarters. I hadn't appreciated how much Carlos protected me from them until he no longer did. They weren't allowed to mark me, which was a relief, and they had to use protection, but nothing in the world, no leash or food bowl could put me in my place like being fucked by ten guys in a day against my will. Not that I had put up a fight, of course. I wasn't that stupid.

But in all, it went easier than it could have gone. Carlos had a soft touch when it came to subjugation. He latched a collar onto me. I whimpered helplessly, and already I could see him softening toward me. He spanked me. He fucked me. He told me to pee in the corner. Then he shoved my face in it. At least he didn't make me lick it up.

That was how I spent my day, chained to a desk. There were worse ways to spend an afternoon. At least I could look outside, enjoy the sunlight through the tinged glass panes. Hell, I really was becoming a dog.

I was only nervous about other guys touching me.

Sure I traded in sex, but I clung to the illusion that I had a choice about my partners. Carlos called me picky, but I didn't like being forced.

A lot of the guys leered at me when we passed in the halls and touched me when they had half a chance. They were willing to use me for sex if given the opportunity. Trunk, in particular, seemed to have a thing for me.

He'd fucked me more than a few times the last time I'd been a puppy. He wasn't into pain, that much I knew, but he did like anal and he was a big guy. At first he put it in without any lube which was excruciating, but I wasn't allowed to talk. I couldn't even beg him for lube. I whimpered and whined—all natural, by the way. At some point the whole animal act really embedded itself in my bones, so communicating by wordless sounds came naturally.

He got the idea, though, when he was done and his dick was covered in blood. The times after that, and there were many in only a week, he'd used plenty of lube, thank God. But he was still a big guy, and it was going to hurt no matter what.

He came to me later and apologized. It was weird but also…nice. That was a whore's version of Hallmark. *I'm sorry for reaming your ass.*

Trunk practically panted when he walked into the office and saw me bound and gagged. He knelt down in front of me, working at the bindings. Well, sure, even he'd have a hard time getting his dick in a pretzel. *No.* I didn't want this. I never had, but somehow it seemed to matter now. My body seemed worth something, more than a bed and clothes anyway.

"Shhh." Thick fingers pinched at my skin, working at the knots. "I got you."

Clever Carlos. Every tug of the rope trapped my breasts tighter, cutting off the blood. I already couldn't feel anything in them which meant there'd be a hell of a lot of pain when I was released. Between my legs, the abrasive rope scrubbed at my inner lips and clit. The point of it all was to punish me if I squirmed, but Trunk was making it worse.

He pulled a knife from his pocket. Instinctively I shrunk back.

"I'm not going to hurt you."

Thick tears slid down my cheeks, tears of pain and shame and maybe even rage. The way they thought they owned my body was bad enough. Worse was the way I believed it too.

"Just hold still."

The fast-paced click of shoes on concrete was the sound of my white knight. Trunk pushed me back down onto the floor. Spit hit my butt cheek and was smeared into my asshole. I tensed. Was he trying to do it quickly? He would never finish in time, but the start alone would hurt so badly. I wanted to scream like the animal they had made me.

When the blunt head of his cock pressed against the very, very closed place, I heard Carlos's voice snap, "Get away from her."

"I'm sorry, *jefe*." Trunk immediately backed away. "I thought—"

"I don't pay you to think. Get out."

Trunk acted surprised, and frankly, so was I. Maybe it was just another mind fuck. I was so used to the horror, the humiliation, that it completely threw me to have Carlos act as my defender. Maybe this whole Tyler thing had thrown Carlos as off balance as it had me. It was like he couldn't make up his mind whether he wanted to be Tyler's mentor in the art of slave training, or fight him for possession. Or both. The same qualities that made Tyler a worthwhile student also made him a threat.

Just when I felt relief about the whole thing, Tyler stepped into the room. It was the slight falter in his steps, the tightening of his mouth, and the veiling of his eyes. They told me that he hated seeing my like this and that when he told Carlos I looked fuckable, it was a charade.

As if to dispel any misconceptions that he'd gone soft, Carlos used me extra hard that night. I'd been expecting it, but it still hurt. No matter how much you brace yourself for the pain, it always comes as a shock. He fucked me in all three places which was unusual for him, but maybe he was inspired by Trunk's near miss earlier. I was thoroughly battered, from both the fading bruises of earlier and the new ones he inflicted in bed. Then he fell asleep, into the kind of deep sleep that was exactly what I needed.

I pulled the small gadget from the corner of Carlos's

closet where I'd slipped it. Then I pressed it to his limp thumb, every second like an eternity, imagining a thousand painful deaths. He didn't stir, not a single eyelid. All men looked more vulnerable in their sleep. Some whores I'd met, older women who'd passed through as camp whores, said it was during sex when men were most vulnerable, tempted as they were by women's bodies and their own pleasure.

But those women had never had sex with Carlos. He wasn't tempted by women's bodies or by his own pleasure, not really. He just wanted to humiliate. The whole torture angle was just a bloody cover on the mind fuck that he really got off on. That's why one of those blank-eyed whores never worked. It's why none of the slaves they were importing, no matter how pretty, would last for him. They come from some godforsaken shithole places that didn't even care when their girls went missing. The position of sex slave to a rich guy was actually a step up.

Carlos wanted his girls from here because we expected freedom. It was ingrained into us, the expectation for respect and equality, making it that much harder to give it all up. He wanted a woman to hope for happiness through all the pain. Deep, soul-searing pain was his kink.

The joke was on him. It had been a long time since I'd expected anything else.

CHAPTER EIGHT

A FTER A QUICK stop to freshen up in my bathroom and dress in actual clothes, I went to Tyler's room. It should be a quick drop-off. He probably needed to get the thumbprint to whatever tech guys were going to work on it.

And I had no business fraternizing with a man who would break my heart. But it was only business, not pleasure. What a crock. It was the only pleasure I'd had all day, the sight of his tense face when he opened the door.

I opened my mouth to tell him that I'd gotten the print, to stop feeling like an idiot, but he pulled me inside before I could speak, jamming his mouth onto mine. It was rough and bruising, which should have been par for the course, but somehow felt totally unfamiliar. Like he wanted *me*, not a body. Like he claimed me and cherished me at the same time.

"God, I'm sorry. I'm sorry," he murmured against my skin.

Tears took me by surprise, springing into my eyes and falling down my cheeks. I had made it through a full day of humiliation and pain not shedding a single tear.

Why should I cry when he was kind to me?

I didn't want him to be sorry. I didn't want to cry.

"I got it. The print," I said, my voice thick with emotions I didn't want to name.

"Good." He looked miserable, not pleased.

It was better this way, with Tyler knowing exactly what I was and what kind of sick shit I did for Carlos. It would help me keep my own feelings at bay, now that I knew he was disgusted by me. Though the thick ridge pressing into my stomach said he was anything but disgusted.

I should have been appalled. Or offended. Anything but horny, but there it was.

I wasn't that familiar with arousal, which was weird, considering. I knew what it looked like on a man, how it felt and how it hurt. But I was cold as stone. Even now it wasn't heat that buzzed through me. More like longing. Uncomfortably like hope.

I dashed that thought quickly, but suddenly, I wanted to fuck him. We could call it lust. We could call it convenience. I was feeling just wired up enough, just careless enough to initiate it.

Of course it would hurt. If he so much as breathed on my body in the state it was in, it would hurt like hell. But that was sex. I was used to it. I just wanted to see if maybe, possibly, it could be different with Tyler. I wanted to know what it would be like to have sex with a guy I …well, the man that I had come to care about. I could be honest here and now, riding this adrenaline high. God knew time was running out.

And the fact that he didn't love me back, that he knew I was a disgusting whore, that was all the better. He wouldn't get wrapped up in a fairytale that didn't have any hope of coming true.

Still with my back to the door, I dropped to my knees in front of him. My knees screamed in protest, bruised as they were, but I ignored them, putting my hands to the bulge, unbuttoning.

"Christ." He grabbed my hands, held them still, but didn't move them away. I could feel his indecision tightening his grip, as if he wanted me but wished he didn't. I knew all about that.

A frisson of shame raced along my skin, sharpening my arousal. He didn't want me. It couldn't be more clear. But the vision, the fantasy, held me enthralled. Maybe I could have it. I didn't need it to be real. I only needed tonight. I'd make it good for him.

"Please." I looked up at him, begged him. "Just pretend. Pretend you love me."

"Oh, hell," he said as his eyes closed. He looked like he was in pain, real pain.

"Only for tonight. I won't expect more."

"It shouldn't be like this for us," he mumbled, but his hands loosened just a fraction.

"I'll do what you ask," I whispered. "I'll get out when Carlos leaves. I'll go to Zachary."

His eyes snapped open, and I knew he understood what I just offered and all that it implied. That I had planned on getting myself killed, despite what he had said about running off to Zachary. But if I could just have this, this pretend fairytale night, then I would do what he wanted. I'd live.

I could only hope the trade would be worth it in the end.

"Come." He picked me up off the floor, and I thought he was rejecting me, but it was only the blowjob he rejected. With a solemnity more appropriate to a funeral, he led me to the bed and laid me down. I tried to hold back my gasp when my back touched the bed, but he heard it anyway and turned me gently onto my stomach.

I groaned. This wasn't part of the dream. Lovers didn't do it doggy-style, did they?

But this wasn't doggy style. This wasn't anal. This wasn't anything I was familiar with, as he breathed feather-light kisses along my hairline and down my jaw. His hands trailed after his mouth, as if he were desperate to touch me all over, everywhere. I luxuriated in the illusion.

My hands scrabbled at the sheets and held on as his mouth dipped lower, down the back of my neck. Shivers rippled all the way down my spine, pain and pleasure.

"Mia," he said softly.

I moaned, unable to speak but praying it wasn't over. Praying it would never end.

"Mia," he repeated. "You're beautiful. You are."

His finger drew the silhouette of my face, starting

from the bridge of my nose, down to brush across my lips. I believed him, not out of vanity, though I'd been told that enough times to think it was true. I was thankful he thought so. Thankful my appearance brought him pleasure.

Slowly, so slowly, he peeled the clothes off me, tenderly lifting each limb as he did so. He kissed each place, each patch of skin he uncovered. God, he was so good at this. He was so good at pretending that I couldn't imagine the real thing feeling any better.

He skipped over the bruises and the welts, only sucking in a sharp breath or muttering a curse at the worst ones. That tarnished the illusion, the fact that my body had to be so broken for this. But I was running out of time with him. We had to do it now or we never would.

His fingers found me wet, already bucking into the blanket. I'd come plenty of times. And with men, too, not just by my own hand. People thought that whores didn't get off, but that wasn't true. Carlos would make me come if he thought it would increase my humiliation. Trunk had made me come, too, back when he'd taken me anally, though it hurt more than felt good when my ass clenched around his thick cock. Even as a child….no, I wouldn't think about that. Not when Tyler's hands were on me, in me. I only had this one time, already slipping through my fingers, to replace all of those memories.

As he pressed a certain spot, I cried out and pushed my hips down hard.

"Yes," he said. "Just like that, baby. Take what you need."

I did, pushing and moaning in rhythmical gulps of pleasure until I shuddered in his arms. I lay there, sated. Yes, this was what lovers did. Maybe the position was different because of my back, but what he'd done with his hands was all about giving, not taking. Foreign and beautiful, like some Asian scroll I could marvel at but never understand.

He wasn't done with me. Though I felt boneless, he propped me up against the headboard so that I faced it and held on. Then he maneuvered his way underneath me so that his head was beneath my cunt. The first touch of his tongue, the first touch of *any* tongue there, sent a shock through me. It wasn't even lust at that point. It was like the cool kiss of silk or the warmth of chicken soup. It was everything luxurious and comfortable all at once.

His tongue touched every part of me as he moaned right along with me. The pressure climbed and held right at the edge, until a firm suck on my clit sent me over. It wasn't flying. It was like sinking, unable to breathe but not caring at all.

I wriggled back to life, sure that I needed to get off him, to thank him profusely for what he'd done, probably with my mouth. But his hands clamped down on my thighs, holding me there, and with soft, small licks, he built me up all over again.

Again and again, he made me come. I was adrift in

pleasure, tossed by its waves and drowning down, down, but unable to care. Something tugged me back though, a shudder in the body beneath me, an urgent sound interspersed with the moans of arousal. I glanced back to see him gripping his cock. Not the fist of bringing himself off, but a harsh, tight thing that turned his knuckles white. He was holding his orgasm at bay in a way that had to be painful, just so that I could keep doing this. So that this could be about me and not his pleasure. He knew exactly what I needed. He knew everything.

I yanked myself off of him. His face was lined with pain, a sight that filled me with guilt and sympathy…and some pleasure. Maybe some of Carlos's sadism had rubbed off on me, because in that moment it felt just a little bit good that he'd been willing to go through that for me.

But I had no interest in prolonging his torture. I rolled a condom on his straining cock and straddled him. I rode him in the way that he would enjoy the most and come the fastest. It was working, too. He looked fair to bursting, with veins bulging in his forehead and almost a snarl on his face.

But he stopped me. "No, no, baby. Let me show you."

With his hands on my hips, he moved me differently. He didn't go as deep or get fucked as well. But the angle—God, the angle. It hit something inside me, something I barely knew I had. Once, twice, I rolled my hips just to hit it again even as my eyes rolled to the back of my head. I felt the wetness spilling down over his cock, my breasts bouncing in time with my movements, but all I could think of was *again* and *more* and *oh God.*

I came and started up all over again. I could tell he was trying to stay still, trying to let me lead, but he bucked beneath my anyway. Just as I came again, clenching around him, he yanked me down with a roar, holding my body suspended in the air as he pummeled me from below as he came.

I fell down onto him as he released me.

"I love you," he said into my neck. "I love you, Mia."

The words struck right at my heart, turning my body cold. It was exactly what I'd asked of him, but I hated it. He was better at faking this than I would have thought. Better than I was even. I'd gotten lost in the moment, thought it was real. Until he said those words, words I knew could never be true, and it all came crashing back to me.

I couldn't believe I'd made him fuck me like that. Was he disgusted by me? He should be.

I had no cause to ever complain about my lot as a whore, even in my head. Because the fact was that as soon as I'd wanted someone and had the means to force him, I'd done it. I made Tyler use his body to get what he needed just like Carlos made me use mine.

Jerkily, I pulled off the bed and grabbed my clothes. I relished each stab of pain from the fabric as it snagged on my open wounds, knowing I deserved even worse.

"What is it?" His chest was still heaving, and his eyes were still bleary and sated as he looked at me.

I shook my head. It wasn't his fault. I wanted to tell him that, explain that it was me that had screwed him over, that he shouldn't feel any shame about what happened, but my mouth wouldn't form the words. And he'd done it for me. Even if I forced him into it, he'd pleased me and I wanted him to know how much it meant to me, at least.

"Thank you," I finally choked out. "Thank you for doing this."

Then I fled the room.

CHAPTER NINE

ALL MEN LIKED blowjobs, but Carlos had a special affinity to them, particularly the choking, gagging kind. That's what I was doing with my head between Carlos's legs when Tyler walked in. My leaking eyes had surely made my mascara run, and the entire bottom half of my face was covered with saliva and pre-cum. Even without a mirror, I was disgusted with myself. I was almost grateful for the thick cock in my mouth, shielding the ugly sight of my face as it did.

Tyler cleared his throat. "I need to have a word with you."

Thank you for doing this, I mocked myself ruthlessly with the words I'd spoken to Tyler last night. So polite. We could write an etiquette column for the gangbanger set.

"Yes, come in," Carlos said impatiently. "Ignore her."

God, if only Tyler *could* ignore me. I wouldn't be offended. I'd be grateful. But I was pretty sure it was impossible. Not only because of the loud, messy blowjob, made worse by Carlos's hand ramming my mouth onto him, harder and deeper, but because of the slutty get-up I'd worn to entice Carlos into using me. The draping top, just a wisp of fabric, showed off the scars on my back. Carlos liked to see them.

From the corner of my eye, I saw Tyler perch on a nearby chair, as awkward as a choir boy watching his first porno. He'd give himself away like that. No bona fide human trafficker had a problem watching a slut get roughed up. He might as well flash his FBI badge. We were both losing our ability to fake it, which was the only thing keeping an undercover agent and a whore alive.

I needed to distract Carlos before he made Tyler for a cop.

I sucked in deep, far back into my throat where I couldn't breathe, not even through my nose. My lips kissed the base of his cock, my face smashed into his stomach. Then I swallowed, gratified by the low masculine groan that reverberated through the air and through his cock. Gratified because it gave Tyler a chance to compose himself.

Unfortunately, he didn't take the hint.

"I want to go over the schematics one last time before tomorrow's run," Tyler said. "Let's take it into the office."

God*damn*, I knew what he was doing. Exactly what I was doing. He was trying to distract Carlos to give me a break. But hell, I didn't need a break from this. This was all I was good for. This was all I could offer Tyler, the services of a slut.

"Sure," Carlos said, as if he was finishing up a card game or something instead of shoving his dick into a throat. "Hold on."

He pushed me down deep again and held me there. My body instinctively jerked and flailed in a futile attempt to get free, even though I told it not to. If I managed to get free, it would only result in more pain for me. So thank goodness Carlos was strong enough to hold me down. Thank goodness for that.

"Stop," Tyler barked.

Carlos froze. His thigh muscles tensed, his fingers tightened in my hair, holding me still, but it wasn't the moment of climax, it was an unnatural stillness. An animal sensing danger.

"What did you say to me?" Carlos asked.

"We don't have time for this," Tyler said. I could tell he was trying to calm down, trying to play it cool, but he was failing fast. "That's all. We need to go."

Carlos was no fool. He pulled my head off his dick and held it there, suspended by my hair, like he was some kind of conquering Visigoth regarding the detached head of his vanquished enemy with pride and scorn. Except, of course, that my head was still attached to my body. But I was no less conquered, no less damaged than if my body were broken in two.

The shame that had nipped at my heels my entire life overtook me completely, flattened me, as I was humiliated in front of the man that I…loved. I'd loved him ever since he'd thought a gangly little girl in dirty clothes was worth standing up for, even if it hadn't worked.

"I don't think you're upset about the security schematics," Carlos said pleasantly. "We went over them last night, and nothing has changed. I think you want me to stop shoving my dick down her throat. Now why would that be?"

Tyler said nothing, but the tension swirled around us, threatening to drag me under. It was a tangible thing: Tyler's impotent rage, his misdirected fury, weighty and thick.

Carlos's sharp tone sliced through the air. "Do you like her?" He shook my head with a flick of his wrist. "Do you like my whore?"

"You know I do," Tyler said. "I offered you a fair price."

I thought with despair that Tyler *did* like me. Maybe it wasn't just that he was a good guy. Maybe it wasn't that he felt guilt over back then or now. Maybe he genuinely thought I was a regular person, worthy of his possession.

Carlos let go, and I fell to the floor like a worthless sack of flour, the dust rising around me in protest. "Take her if you want," he said. "But if you leave, don't come back. You won't participate in the drop. You forfeit your cut."

Freedom.

For a second, just a second, I allowed myself to revel in the possibility. Tyler and me, together. Happiness, a family. Life flashed before my eyes, one I'd never live. A fantasy.

The offer was a trick.

No way would Carlos let me go. I'd known that ever since the first time he shot down one of his men in front of me.

I'd been new here, barely off the streets for six weeks. As embarrassing as it was to acknowledge, I'd even developed a romantic attachment to Carlos. Well, maybe it wasn't so ridiculous. He was very intelligent and attractive enough, if you couldn't see the monster underneath. And he was my knight in shining armor. The age difference between us didn't matter to me. Maybe I did have daddy issues.

He'd fucked me on his bed—this was before he got too rough. Maybe he thought that I'd run then, even with nowhere to go. And I might have, without those delusional romantic feelings.

One of his men walked in on us. I saw him first and made a surprised squeak. Carlos looked over, his hard cock still inside me, grabbed the gun from the drawer in the bedside table and shot him dead. Then he went back to fucking me with fervor.

I started crying, but that only excited him more. He finished and then called in Leo to clean up the mess. A dead body. Very little blood. The smell of piss. I'd never forget any of it. I found out later that the guy had been skimming off the top. Only a fool would steal from Carlos. The man had already been dead when Carlos shot him, that's how inevitable his death was.

Still, I thought that he'd done it in front of me on purpose. It signaled a change in our relationship. We were no longer a starry-eyed girl and her savior—he owned me. He showed me exactly what he'd do if I ever left, if I ever betrayed him. So I had no illusions that he'd let me leave now, even if he said I could.

Probably Tyler knew too much to let loose, either. If he tried to get me out of here now, we'd both be dead before we hit the parking lot. I looked up at Tyler, trying to warn him, begging him to hold back. His eyes were haunted, filled with rage and guilt and disgust and all manner of dark things. But he obeyed, staying still.

Carlos stood, giving the impression of a dog crouching over his bone. "That is what I thought. Just because I shared her with you, don't forget who she belongs to."

He ripped apart the flimsy silk fabric of my shirt and pulled the knife from his shirt pocket. The metal touched my skin, cold and merciless. Carlos wasn't even looking at me. He was looking at Tyler as he carved a curved line across my stomach. The blade curved back around, snaking into the letter C. For Carlos, maybe, or cunt. Or cold, because my body started to shiver. The thoughts faded like smoke into the ether as my body's responses took over. The pain seared through me, imprinted itself on my mind and in my heart. An inside hurt to match the thick scar this would leave.

Carlos didn't like to do permanent damage. He liked a clean slate to work with when he beat me. This was another message that I wouldn't be around for long.

My body convulsed, desperate for a safety that my mind knew would never come. I couldn't breathe, couldn't hope for the moment the pain would ease. The room refocused, veiled in a red sheen of agony. Tyler's stony silence pulsated in the room. He did it for me.

"I don't know why you're shitting bricks," Carlos said. "You're the one who told me about her."

I blinked through the miasma of misery to make sense of his words. What had Tyler told Carlos about me? Tyler didn't know anything about me, except maybe about where I grew up. Though in reality, Carlos probably had a better understanding of what had gone on behind closed doors than Tyler, because that's the kind of understanding guy he was.

Wait. Tyler also knew I was working as an informant. It made sense now, too much sense. Carlos had been exceptionally brutal. I knew why. I was dispensable. A traitor. Like the guy who'd stolen from him, I was already dead.

A mournful wail blanketed us, that universal sound of an animal in pain. It made my hair stand on end. It made my throat burn as it left me. It wasn't that I was dead or dying. It was because Tyler had ratted me out. His bowed head screamed his guilt.

"Oh, yes," Carlos said. "I know what you are. What you did. Did you really think I wouldn't find out? Did you think you could fuck with me?"

"No," I whispered, and then realized it was true. I always knew he'd win this game. He was too good at it. It was all he could do, really. Like an idiot savant, except instead of playing piano or counting cards, his genius was fucking with people. But I'd hoped to be able to free those women, at least, before he found me out.

Now their only hope was Tyler, except I didn't know whose side he was on anymore. Why had he betrayed me? But that's how fucked up I was, that I had expected anything different.

"Don't play innocent now. Tell her," Carlos said with a ringmaster's sweep of his arm.

"Fuck, Mia," he said. Or I was pretty sure he said that. It also sounded like *fuck me*. They meant the same thing though. *Oops. My bad. Sorry about the whole torture/death thing.*

"Just...why?" I said, the tears in my eyes twisting his face like a funhouse mirror.

"Well, Tyler, tell her what she wants to hear," Carlos said.

He mumbled something. An apology maybe. It didn't matter.

I struggled to sit up. I had this urge to storm from the room in a huff. Probably it was the blood loss making me have visions, but I imagined this scene where I was a normal woman. "You came home late and didn't even call," I'd say and then go putter around in the kitchen until we could kiss and make up. But this was nothing like that, and besides, I couldn't really move, so I ended up flopping heavily onto the concrete.

I'd never understood that about fishing, how they could just let them die slowly, suffocating and writhing. We wanted to be put out of our misery. We just couldn't say so.

A sharp pain registered on the side of my head, and then a dark eclipse. Carlos's boot on my face, I realized with detachment. He was saying things about how I was his, and how dare Tyler presume. Tyler asked him to let me go, said that I wasn't important and to focus on the drop. Like the baby in Solomon's judgment, if one of them didn't give soon, I'd split right in two.

Carlos snarled. "You want her so bad then fuck her. Do it or I'll blow her brains out."

Tyler looked ready to beat Carlos to death. And he could do it, but Carlos had a gun pointing at my head, not to mention fail-safes in place, people who would take retribution and both our lives if Tyler were to fight back.

"Please," I gasped.

Carlos stepped back smugly as Tyler knelt beside me.

"Just hold on." His eyes beseeched me to understand things I didn't. "Let me take you out of here. I don't care about the drop."

"No." I shook my head, wishing I had more air. I wished with all my inconsiderable might that he were still a good guy, a good cop, but either way he had to go. Taking me with him would put him at risk. "Not too deep. I'll be fine. Do what he says."

"No. No fucking way."

It was the only way. Why couldn't he see that?

"Please," was all I could say, trying to infuse it with everything I couldn't.

A long pause bloated with pain and worry, but then I

felt gentle hands lift my skirt. I could have sighed in relief if I hadn't been breathing through the pain. It was like Lamaze, breathing evenly so as not to scream. It was a form of labor, after all. Getting tortured was hard work.

His eyes glued to the mess of blood on my stomach, he pulled out his cock, soft and limp. His limbs moved mechanically, as if he were entranced. Maybe he was in shock. Even for a tough guy soldier and cop, this was sick stuff.

Whatever he was, he wasn't aroused. He went to put it in and the soft skin just rubbed up against me, as if shrinking away from me. Well, I couldn't blame it for that, but neither could I let it happen. There was only one way for this to end, and that was with Tyler walking away safely.

I managed to prop myself up, managed not to wail as the skin and muscle pulled apart a little more. Then I reached for his cock and stroked it with a practiced hand.

"Hey," I whispered. "Look at me."

He looked up at my eyes. I flinched at what was in his eyes, my own pain reflected back.

"It's okay. I liked what we did before." I struggled to keep my voice even, not to betray what this was costing me. "I like your body, so hard and rough. And I think you like mine, when it's not all messed up like now. My breasts, my cunt. Just think about that. Think about me in your bed, all sexy and pure."

It was all a lie of course. Well, not the part about me liking him, but the idea that I was pure. Still, it worked, and between my words and the physical touch, he was half-erect. It was enough to put him in, and from there, my body would do the work. It even clenched all on its own, as the pain throbbed through my stomach, as if it were built just for men to hurt and fuck in tandem.

His thrusts were short, jerky things that quickly ended in release. I would have thought he was faking it if I hadn't felt warmth bathe me below. A glance showed that Carlos wasn't suspicious. Instead he looked curious, almost bemused, as if he didn't quite understand what he was watching even though he was the one who ordered it.

In the silence that followed, Carlos laughed with a maniacal ring. I couldn't fathom what was funny, even in a twisted sense. "You have a little crush. You wanted your dick in her throat, not mine. Well, you should thank me. You got what you wanted, but the fun is over. Something is wrong here. The air is wrong. Go call the other men. We move the shipment up by one hour."

Tyler didn't move, still hung over me as if he could protect me, shield me from the horror with his body. God, he should know it was too late for that. It had been too late even when I'd known him as a kid. The horror was inside me, calling to the worst part of men.

"Go," I whispered. *Go and be safe. Find someone else, someone normal. Be happy.*

He breathed harshly, unevenly, reminding me of a cornered animal.

"Do it," I urged. "Please."

The harsh ring of Carlos's cell phone was like some macabre soundtrack in our little drama. He turned away to take the call.

"I know this doesn't look good," he whispered. "Just trust me. Just go along with it until this is over, just until the drop and then we'll nail his ass. Please, Mia."

"Okay," I agreed. Anything to keep him from some stupid show of heroics. The relief washed over me like a cool breeze. "Go now. I'll see you after."

The light blinded me as he moved off me, allowing the harsh lights to expose me. Only when I heard the slow thuds of his boots on the concrete growing softer as he walked away did I realize I had hoped he *would* save me. But that's how perverse I was, that I'd wish for Tyler to stay even if it meant his death. Even knowing it was illogical, hope wanted him to care enough to stop this no matter the cost. The tragedy of Romeo and Juliet had never made more sense than right now. Like we'd rather make a dramatic exit together than ever be apart. What crap. Because really, I was alone and hurt. I'd believed him. I trusted him. That was the tragedy.

Give me a little credit, he'd said.

I never wanted to hope, but it clung like vines, strangling the life out of me. The first blow landed on my ribs, echoing inside me, because I was empty, so hollow. The second one hit my shoulder. Mostly Carlos liked to kick me for a good beating. It was easier for him to keep up his stamina. The pain screamed through me in a litany of *stupid, stupid, stupid girl for getting your hopes up, for thinking you were worth something.*

Only when Carlos heaved, out of breath, did I realize that this one was different. I'd die today, soon but not soon enough. I curled up into a ball, uncaring if it made Carlos angrier, maybe even wishing it did. End it sooner. God, please. And then it stopped.

"Leo," I heard him snap. "Get in here."

I shuddered and spasmed on the floor, unable to control my body. These were the moments I wished I were dead, when I was too weak to do anything about it. It was nature's cruel irony, stringing me along.

"Keep going with her," Carlos said.

A short pause. "She looks pretty messed up already."

"Do what I fucking say," Carlos snapped. "Everyone's a critic today. I know you want to rip her pretty skin. You want to smear the blood all over her. I can see it in your eyes. Don't forget that I know you, Leo. Do it now. I'm waiting."

The caress of leather on fabric signaled Leo's belt leaving his pants. He put up a good fight against his sadism, but I was like an open bar to an alcoholic. Carlos's words had inflamed him. I couldn't look. I didn't have the strength to turn my head anyway.

A lash hit, and then another. It felt like every hit propelled me across the floor, jerking and gasping, but I was staying still. I knew by the pool of blood and other questionable liquids that grew and grew. It was just like Carlos said—skin ripping and blood smearing.

"I'm going to the meeting," Carlos said. "Have some

fun with her. Take your time and then dispose of her."
He bent down over me, a grin lighting his face. "I lied,
you know. He was the one who gave you two away. He
was too interested in you, too interested in a used up
whore."

The one who gave you two away. The two of us, as if
he'd learned both our secrets instead of just mine. The
shock must have registered on my face even through the
bruises, because he laughed.

"Don't worry, *cara*," he said. "He'll pay for that."

Then the door shut, and I was left in Leo's care.

Chapter Ten

THE BELT DROPPED in front of my face.

"Thank God he's gone," Leo said. The hoarseness in his voice wasn't from exertion. He could beat a man with his fists for hours before tiring. Maybe it was guilt, but my guess was arousal.

The man got so turned on by pain, by a sliced up woman. It wasn't his fault. He really couldn't control it. But I couldn't tell him so. Couldn't move my jaw at all. It might have been broken.

He knelt beside me. His touch was gentle like Tyler's, but where Tyler had avoided my cuts and bruises, Leo traced them. They burned from the salt of his skin.

"What'd you do?" His voice held regret, but also a morbid acceptance that he liked it anyway, that he would take what he could get. It was always my fault.

I gave a short shake of my head against the concrete which only succeeded in dizzying me. I didn't think I had much in the way of consciousness left.

"I'm not going to hurt you anymore. I'm not." It sounded like he was trying to convince himself, and failing. "You've been through enough."

Some shuffling sounds came to my ear, the very air

rustled, and then an even softer touch pricked my open wounds. He was licking me, I realized, tasting my blood, feeling the jagged skin against his tongue. I hated my body for appealing to him, for attracting him, but at least this was passive. When Leo hurt me, I could take myself away in my mind. Carlos never allowed that.

I couldn't hope that he'd disobey Carlos, not when he'd never done it before, but I could try. "Please, just make it quick. Give me the knife, I'll do it. Please."

He shook his head thoughtfully. "I'm not going to kill you."

That's how I knew I was in a bad way, that those words inspired disappointment instead of relief. "Why not?" Petulant little girl, bleeding on the floor.

"I need your help." Light flickered in his eyes and then extinguished—the light of sanity. "There's going to be a new *jefe* around here. Carlos has gotten out of hand. And Tyler…" He made a low sound of dismissal.

He was hardly the first person to challenge Carlos for leadership. Honestly, I didn't think he had it in him, not to win, not even to try, but maybe Tyler had really gotten to him.

"A few of the guards are with me already. The rest will scatter when the fighting starts. Carlos and his pretty boy Tyler don't stand a chance."

I tried to process this. Maybe Leo didn't have it in him to actually run this place, but if he'd prepared a trap…

"Why would you need me?" I asked.

"Tyler's one of my guys. He's going to take down Carlos there, and in return, I turn over a few big time guys and get immunity. Well, fuck that. I've been under Carlos's thumb for too long to take orders from some fuckwad FBI agent. Once Carlos is dead and Tyler has control of the shipment, you're my trump card."

I laughed. The sound in my throat when I heard how crazy it sounded. Maybe Tyler had betrayed me to Carlos. Or maybe he hadn't since Carlos seemed to know about both of us. But even if he hadn't, even if this was part of some twisted plan of his to free the slaves, to get me out, to get a promotion, he didn't give a shit about me. "Tyler doesn't want me."

Leo gave me a kick in the ribs, almost a friendly admonition, like a light punch in the arm. "You stupid girl. What do you think this is all about?"

I thought back to when Tyler had asked to buy me. Carlos had refused again and again. Did Tyler really want me as his whore that badly?

Leo shook his head. "You don't get it. He came here looking for you. That's how I first found him out, sniffing around for a Mia who grew up on the southside. Brown hair, that's all he knew. I was just going to blow his brains out, you know, just to keep him out of Carlos's business. But he's real eager to talk to you, see if you're okay or some shit. That made me laugh, you know, because look at you, but I figured if he wanted access that badly, I could use him."

I blinked up at the rafters, my eyes finally dry. I was

all messed up from the beating, still smarting over the betrayal. That had to be why this wasn't making any sense. He'd come here for me?

"Yeah, he has it bad." Leo looked me up and down, unimpressed. "I guess you're not that messed up. For a whore." He pulled out his half-erect cock with a helpless shrug. "There's still time."

I shut my eyes against the yellow stream, but the hot slap against my skin and the acrid smell assaulted me just the same. My skin would've crawled if it weren't already burning from the acidic wash. I was already going to be his meal ticket. Did I really need to get literally pissed on, too? But that's Leo for you.

LEO GAVE ME a few minutes to wash off in the shower and put on some wet clothes. He wasn't being considerate. We'd made it all the way downstairs before he sniffed, probably realizing he'd be stuck in the car with me covered in cooling piss.

"In." He nodded me toward my bathroom.

I stripped my clothes without modesty, eager to let the scorching hot water burn away the memories. That was one of the great things about being housed in this industrial complex, the hotel-like water heater. Even as large as it was, I probably used up most of the hot water. But I was often the only girl around here, and I figured that garnered me some privileges despite my lowly status.

When I stepped out of the shower, Leo wasn't in the

bedroom anymore. I heard his low murmurs coming from the hallway. Where other women's counters might be stocked with lotions and powders, I had disinfectant and antibiotic creams. With a quickness born of practice, I cleaned the cut on my stomach—fuck, it burned—and some of the bigger scrapes. Then I used extra-large butterfly tape to seal the cut closed.

I'd heard about those liquid stitches, where you could paint it over the wound like white-out, but they didn't carry them at my usual online pharmacy which was set up with illegal pain meds and Carlos's credit card. Speaking of which, I popped a couple of pain pills. I was feeling a little light-headed, I thought. Yes.

I started as I realized I was staring at the wall.

Fucking blood loss.

Leo was still on the phone, so I went to my dresser. I didn't get my own cell phone, seeing as I was only allowed outside the compound with Carlos or Leo, but I had Zachary's phone.

Static cracked through the earpiece so loudly I was sure Leo would come charging in. "Hello?" came Zachary's voice, small and tinny.

"Zachary, it's me," I whispered.

"Hello?" he said again, a little louder now but obviously he hadn't heard me. Damn.

I went back into the bathroom and flipped on the shower for white noise. "Zachary? Can you hear me?"

"Mia, what's going on? Are you okay?"

What a loaded question. Although the answer was

simple enough—*no*. "I'm fine. Listen, how did Tyler get this job?"

"Who? Listen, we've got a problem. My guy's gone off the grid. What's happening over there? The drop isn't supposed to be for a few days."

A chill caressed over me like a slick blade. "It's been moved up. I'm talking about Tyler. Tyler Martinez. Your guy."

"No, he's Jack Martin."

More crackling buzzed from the earpiece, or maybe it was only in my head. The shadows closed in on me.

"Wait," he said. "I thought you made him. Oh, but that's not the name he goes by undercover. It's Trunk."

Without a word, I dropped the phone into the toilet with a plop, slammed the lid shut, and fell. Blackness folded me in its embrace before I even hit the tile.

I MUST BE on a ship, I thought. I was both lulled and nauseated by the endless rocking, back and forth. Back and forth. I gagged and choked on a thick wad of fabric. That should have been the end. I should have vomited into the small space and suffocated on my own bile. But my body was too damn good at surviving, always had been. With a shudder, it tamped down the urge to throw up, leaving me with a faint sickly feeling.

The shiny plastic ceiling puzzled me. It felt like hours that I stared at it, thoroughly befuddled. What kind of room was so very short? It looked like the roof to one of those Barbie limos, but white. Surely, I hadn't died and turned into a Barbie doll.

Every degree my neck turned wrenched down my spine, until finally I stared at small round windows. Holy fuck, I really was on a ship. I'd thought that was just medication-fueled fancy. Although ship was probably too fine a word for the thin plastic walls and dirt-scuzzed port windows. Still, they were round. Very ship-like, very authentic, I thought, unaccountably pleased at that fact.

Damn, I needed sleep. Now I had both the pain and the meds swirling around in my mind. *Focus.* The glass, or more likely plastic, was too fuzzy to see out of, but it still let in the dusky light.

"You're up," Leo said. "The show will be starting soon."

I tried to whip my head around but only ended up shutting my eyes on a groan.

"Yeah, you're a mess," he said, almost cheerfully. "Thought you'd offed yourself for a minute there with those pills. But if you tried to, you failed."

Asshole. I groaned.

He chuckled. "Don't worry. You'll get your wish by the end of the night."

Promises, promises. The blackness consumed me again.

❖   ❖   ❖

WHEN I WOKE again, I was still on the boat. But the purr of the motor had ended, leaving only ringing silence in its wake. The portholes said it was darker, as well.

But I was alone. I kicked a few times, hoping to draw Leo's attention. After he didn't come, I realized it was stupid to draw his attention anyway.

There wasn't much I could do bound as I was. And it wasn't just the lack of sounds I heard. It was a stillness in the air. Whatever latent animal senses I possessed told me I was alone.

Alone did not mean safe, however. The place was different, my captor was different, but the trapped feeling was too familiar. My mind flashed back to the metal cage.

"Eat your kibble, eat it all up."

"Not a sound out of you. Bad dogs get their hides whipped."

"Be a good bitch and go on your newspaper. Come on, you won't get out of there until you do it."

Hell, now I had to pee.

And anyway, I couldn't just lie here and wait for fate to fuck with me again. Tyler was out there, the scheming, lying bastard. If I was going down, then I was getting answers out of him first. If not that, then I figured I could nail a kick to the balls. I'd pay for it after, but it'd be worth it.

I struggled to sit up. My breath caught at what I saw. Maybe I had underestimated Leo. He could be a decent replacement for Carlos after all, because I found that though my ankles and wrists were still bound, a knife winked at me from the cracked plastic bench. And between me and that bench was a thick layer of glass. I'd have to walk, or crawl, on broken glass to get free. It was like a macabre fairytale, except instead of a red carpet there was a carpet of glass, and instead of a prince there was a knife. The same principle.

With a wrench in my side, I maneuvered myself to a sitting position and inched my way across the floor in the slowest escape ever. I found that if I slid my butt through the glass, instead of over it, that saved me a lot of glass splinters. Still, there was no avoiding the cuts all over my ankles as I dug in and gained enough leverage to pull my ass along the floor.

Luckily, the pain in my bloodied feet was barely noticeable. Not over the breath-stopping pain in my stomach. I swore if I made it out of there alive, I'd die. There'd been a time that had seemed like a release, like freedom. Maybe it still held a certain allure, but I had unfinished business. Maybe I really was already dead, and I was just a ghost trying to wrap up the loose ends. A bloody, weary ghost whose uncontainable groans of agony tangled with the wind that gently rocked the boat.

Finally I reached the bench and hauled my ass up, wincing at the piercings of glass into my soles. My fingers fumbled for the knife, scraping and sawing until finally my hands were free. By the time I got to work on my ankles, blood had pooled at my feet, slithering under the glass to form a red sequined blanket. It was pretty, I conceded, the glittering blanket of suffering. That might have been the pain meds talking.

I glanced behind me out the porthole and barely made out lights bobbing in the distance. Or maybe the lights were stationary and this boat was the one bobbing. Slipping over my own blood, walking on my own cuts, I hobbled out of the cabin and onto the small deck. The ocean marked me with its spray, salty and thick, as I leaned over the railing. Away from me, dark swirls circled and threatened, but up close to the boat, they lapped disarmingly. Which was the true nature of the sea, the murky monster or the gentle lover? Maybe both, which was almost a scarier thought, because in the end, it didn't matter. I was lost to them both.

I jumped. Cold water filled my mouth, my nose. Salt burned my feet, my stomach, all over. Like the lashes of a thousand jellyfish, they stung me into paralysis. I gulped water. I breathed it. I sank.

CHAPTER ELEVEN

I'D SURRENDERED TO the dark mistress, to death. It turned out I wasn't good enough, not even to die. The waves tumbled and scrubbed me like mother nature's washing machine, and then spit me out onto the beach to dry. I clutched at the sand, grounding myself as it clumped wet in my hands.

Lying there, wrung out, I had a memory of another moonlit night.

Dad had come to visit me that night, and then passed out beside my bed. Unable to sleep, to even sit still, I slipped out of the house and into the backyard. The moon had swathed everything in a silver glow. Somehow it wasn't eerie, but peaceful. Like we were all just flat grayscale cutouts in someone's imagination. If we weren't real, then our shame wasn't real either.

I heard noises next door, ones I instinctively recognized, even though I never made them myself. It was the rhythm, the universal rhythm of a man taking. A man hurting. Unable to stem my morbid curiosity, I crept along the peeling wood siding until I reached a window.

Just as I suspected. The man was pushing against a girl underneath him. His hands were all over her, his mouth, his body. And she was making these sounds, breathless and squirming. It had to be hurting her.

Although, oddly, they both seemed to have clothes on. But even as I watched, that was changing. The girl scrabbled at the hem of his shirt. First I thought she was fighting him, maybe pushing him away or scratching at the soft skin there. But then she pulled his shirt off and threw it across the room. Then her hands were back on him, running up and down. And I realized, looking at the slim torso, that it was Tyler. Not his father. Not some faceless, hurting man, but Tyler. And the girl, some made-up slut from school probably.

He was one of them.

It should have been obvious all along, but a whine of shock escaped me. Maybe not surprise, but mourning. Love lost, a love I'd never had.

"Shit," I heard him say.

"What?" the girl asked.

I turned and raced through the dirt and hopped into the old tire, curling up into it. Even over the racing of my heart I heard the screech of the porch door open. The pebbles crunched closer and closer. Tyler's head appeared in my line of vision.

"Hey, little girl," he said softly.

I ignored him.

"I'm sorry you saw that," he said. "I should have closed the window."

I scowled. That wouldn't have changed the fact that he was doing *that*. With her! If he needed to hurt a girl, why couldn't it be me? If I had to be hurt, couldn't I at least choose who hurt me?

"Come out of there," he coaxed. "It's not—"

"No!" I knew what he was going to say, that it wasn't safe. "You don't know anything."

There was a pause, then he said, "Okay, you're right. I don't know. Why don't you come out and you can tell me?"

I didn't care anymore. I wanted him to know just how unsafe I really was. Even then, I knew I could hurt him with that knowledge. So I came out and wielded my weapons: a sensual shimmy inappropriate for my age, a knowing half-smile.

"Do it with me," I whispered.

He cocked his head, all genuine puzzlement. "What?"

"What you were doing with that girl. Do it with me."

He jumped up as if scalded. "Jesus! No!"

The rejection whipped through me. "Fine," I yelled, uncaring if the whole neighborhood heard. Let them!

I stormed off toward the back alley, but he caught my arm in a tight grip and yanked me around. "Mia, I didn't mean it like that."

I refused to look up.

"It's not a personal…you're too young, that's all. Way too young. You're a very pretty girl, and I'm sure—"

"Spare me the pep talk," I growled at him, unwilling

to accept his fake kindness. If he really liked me, thought I was pretty, my age wouldn't matter. I knew that. My age didn't stop them. "I know I'm pretty. I hear it all the time, I'm so pretty. So beautiful and young, and I bet I can make you feel better than she can. I saw her. She couldn't even stay still. I can!"

He stared at me, eyes wide and black. "When—" He swallowed thickly. "When do you stay still?"

The question cut through my reckless temper. I'd said too much. I couldn't think, had to stall. "What?"

"When do you stay still for…that?"

I picked up the pieces of my bravado to boast, "Why? Do you think I don't do it? That no one wants me? Well, not everyone thinks I'm too young."

"Who, Mia? Who doesn't think you're too young?"

He was serious, so serious, and suddenly I had an inkling, a vision of how bad this could get. Already it was spiraling out of my control. "No one." I blinked away the wetness. "I was lying."

"Goddamnit, Mia," he shouted.

The sound of the screen door cut through the night, but it wasn't Tyler's door this time. It was mine.

"What the fuck are you doing out here?" my dad slurred.

This time I didn't wait for Tyler to tell me to go inside. I turned and ran for the steps.

"Stop," Tyler said.

"I told you to stay away from her," my dad said. Then he turned to me. "Get your skinny ass inside."

"No, Mia," Tyler said. "Wait. She was just telling me something."

I started to shiver. Nothing good could come of this. They taught us about Eve in church, how she'd taken a bite of the apple. I thought this was how she must have felt when she realized what it meant. Relieved. Remorseful. Afraid.

They were shouting at each other, hurling so many swear words it was hard to make out a meaning other than fury. Then there was more than words flying through the air, fists and bodies, as they fought. At eighteen, Tyler was strong, but my dad still had a lot of weight on him. The wrestled until finally Tyler had him pinned on the dirt.

My dad spit up into his face. "You don't know shit about shit, you motherfucking cocksucker dickhole shithead."

Tyler lifted him and slammed him against the ground. "You fucker, you disgusting motherfucker. You're going to fucking jail."

I just stood there in shock, but then the girl came running out, screaming and hollering, and I wanted to stop her, to warn her not to bring attention to herself when they were in this rabid state, but I was rooted to the spot.

"Get inside," Tyler said. He hadn't moved his head, but he was talking to the girl.

"But," she whined.

"Do it now," he said. "Just get."

My dad spoke between wheezes as Tyler's forearm pressed into his throat. "That's right, girlie. You don't want my type to catch a look at you. Might be getting ideas." And then he choked out a laugh when she ran inside Tyler's house and slammed the door shut.

But my dad just kept laughing this awful gasping noise that reminded me of an animal dying. Even Tyler seemed freaked out, standing up and releasing him with a shove.

"You... think... you've... got... me?" my dad croaked through his hysteria.

"Fuck you," Tyler said, sounding uncertain.

My dad straightened and made a visible effort to rein himself in. "Boy, I know exactly what your mama is. I done fucked her for some spare change."

Tyler pulled back, preparing to strike.

My dad's arms came up as he spoke quickly. "She ain't legal. I know she don't file shit. An illegal hooker'll get deported as soon as they know her. You say one word against me, and no one will believe you. And you better say goodbye to your mama while you at it."

Tyler's arm was frozen, like the freeze frame in a martial arts movie. His whole body was unmoving. "You fucker."

"That's right." My dad stood taller now, like he'd already won. "A whore in Texas is one thing, but it's still a real life. How long you think she's going to last in Mexico?"

I knew what deported meant. I'd seen kids disappear

from school, deported. Even knowing that, I wanted Tyler to swear at him again, to say he'd protect me no matter what, and his mom too. I could almost hear the words, drifting on the air like a lost melody.

In slow, stiff movements, Tyler backed up a step and dropped his arms. The words wouldn't be coming. My eyes burned and blurred. He couldn't do this to me. Tyler couldn't start a fight with my dad, bring this out into the open, *acknowledge* what was happening, and then leave me to my fate.

It would be so much worse now. Didn't he know my dad would punish me for this? The way Tyler wouldn't meet my eyes told me he knew exactly how I would be punished.

He took another step back, retreating farther away.

"That's right," my dad pressed. "An old, dried up hag like her. She'd get passed around the streets. Probably bleed out the first week there."

Tyler didn't look angry anymore. He looked anguished. Suddenly he didn't look like the savior I'd wished for but the helpless teenage boy he was. I turned and ran into the house. I would rather be in there, even if it meant pain, than face Tyler. I'd thought there was nothing more humiliating than what my dad had done to me. This was worse.

I silently endured under the hands of my father that night and for the nights after that. Tyler disappeared. Not deported. Enlisted. I refused to ask for help, not ever again.

Then I ran away from home. I was barely surviving when Carlos found me. He really had been a savior to me, no matter how tarnished his armor was.

As I grew older, I couldn't hold it against Tyler to protect his own family, his mother, over a stranger. He'd tried to do right by me. He'd tried harder than anyone else. It wasn't his fault that he failed. The irony, that he'd come to claim a used up whore, wasn't lost on me.

Sputtering out the remainder of the ocean's leavings, I dragged myself up. My legs wobbled beneath me as if I were a mermaid who'd emerged from the sea, standing on new legs.

CHAPTER TWELVE

I WAS TOO late. That was what I thought when I looked over the ridge to see a battle scene. Not a battle fought—a battle lost. The men wearing black clothes, face paint, and holsters had clearly subdued the unruly band of mercenaries Carlos hired.

Was Tyler one of the men with their faces pressed into the dirt, cuffed and pinned to the ground? But hope springs eternal, because I frantically scanned the bulky forms of the cops, as if I could recognize Tyler there. Hoping he were one of the good guys after all, that Leo had been wrong.

But I didn't see him anywhere.

I scrambled over the peak to get a closer look but ended up sliding down the embankment. The scrabble of rocks and limbs roared through the salty air, but no one glanced over. I looked again, and this time I was sure. Tyler wasn't here.

Someone else was notoriously absent—or several someones. Where were the women?

The cops seemed to be wondering the same thing. I recognized Zachary talking with some of the men, pointing and gesturing, probably organizing a search.

Most of the cops corralled Carlos's men, but several went off in pairs to search.

The slaves were the prize here. Whether Tyler was good or bad, he would go after them.

I had no hope of finding them before these guys. After all, they knew about this island, they'd have access to maps and would have planned their invasion. I'd had no idea a place like this even existed so close to the city. The harbor was mostly used for yachting and hobbyists, not Lord of the Flies reenactments.

Then I realized I did have some knowledge they didn't. The boat.

After all, Leo had planned some sort of coup with Tyler. So he would have pulled the boat up at an appropriate location. Maybe that was even the meeting site. I raced back up the slope and down the beach where I'd came from. For once, my body was on my side, allowing me to sprint without sluggishness or pain despite my injuries and blood loss. Actually, numbness was more concerning, indicative of scarier things than pain, but I couldn't worry about that now.

At first I thought I'd been wrong, that there was nothing but more darkness. Then I heard a low moan that raised goose bumps on my skin. Every animal can recognize the sound of deathly misery in another. It was coming from the woods beside the beach, and I crept inside.

There, in a clearing, was a straggling line of women. And herding them along was Tyler.

I blinked, wanting to deny it. The women were bound and bruised, with their heads bent low. Tyler urged them along mercilessly, his face stone cold. Leo had been right. Tyler was one of the bad guys. It didn't make sense if he'd come here for me, but as I watched him lead a line of slaves away from the police there could be no doubt.

God, I would have thought I'd have learned by now. Hadn't I made the same mistake with Carlos, thinking he was there to save me when he only wanted to use me? No. *No.*

I tried to formulate a logical play-by-play analysis. How had I missed it? List all the facets of my stupidity, both starting and ending with Tyler. None of it could distract me from the soul-clenching pain of betrayal. It was crippling—almost. Because there was still time to do something about it. I'd set out to free these women, and maybe I still could. Besides the fact that if I did, Tyler would lose. He deserved to lose.

I was no better than he was, using these women for my own purposes. But then again, I didn't think they'd object if it meant they got to be free.

I let the anger grow and roil inside me like one of those burning planets, a tangible fury. How dare he trick me? Lie to me? All he ever had to do was ask. Hell, I'd spent the last several years serving Carlos, and he was no saint. I would have helped Tyler, too, except he hadn't trusted me enough. He'd never trusted me at all.

I had nothing at all to help me, nothing but a rusty

knife and the wrath of a woman scorned. Scratch that. The wrath of several women. There were maybe ten of them on the path, but they stumbled around. It didn't look like any of them were considering escape. Maybe because they knew they would die out there, tied up and naked. Or maybe the ones interested in escape had already been killed.

One of the women near the front tripped. Tyler went to her, and I took my chance. I yanked the straggler in the back to the ground. She shrieked briefly, but I clapped my hand over her mouth.

"Hush. I'm saving you."

Her breath pulsed fast against my fingers, but she didn't squirm or make a sound. We waited in the dirt, both of us heaving, to see if Tyler would have heard us or noticed her absence. When the sound of crunching leaves and crackling branches faded away, I unsnapped the ball gag in her mouth and used the knife to cut away the ropes.

"Who are you?" she asked, her voice hoarse.

"The sorriest excuse for a rescuer, that's who," I muttered.

"We can't leave the other women."

"I wasn't planning on it." I held up the remains of the rope that had only minutes ago been wrapped around her wrists. "Care to return the favor?"

We beelined our way out of the woods onto the beach. It was much faster to move that way, and I guessed Tyler hadn't taken that route to avoid the visibility. We got back to the boat before the rest of the group, and there we set up shop behind a border of brush at the edge of the woods.

The sound of rustling heralded the arrival of Tyler and the other slaves. On cue, the woman burst out of leaves, holding her arms behind her as if they were still tied. She fell to the ground, writhing in feigned pain.

Tyler released the woman he'd been supporting and leaned her against a tree before rushing over. He was greeted with feminine fury in the form of claws and a swift kick to the groin. He fell to his knees, and I, taken over by a crazed madwoman, fell on him from behind.

Even then, even with the element of surprise and two of us against his one, he threw me off and had the woman pinned down. I was furious, furious that he'd won, again. Furious at all the men who kept beating us just because they were bigger and stronger.

Red swathed my vision, blotting out everything except the picture of the man straddling the woman. The knife was in my hand, and then it was stabbed into his side, where he slumped over.

"Oh God, Oh God," I muttered uselessly. What had I done? So much for my hopes to save Tyler, to *be* with him. I'd just killed him.

Frantic, mindless, I pulled the knife from him, as if I could hit the undo button on my moment of insanity, but that only made the blood spurt. I pushed the edges of his shirt down. He groaned and writhed, but at least he wasn't dead yet.

The woman ran back to me, though I hadn't realized she'd even gone. "We've got to get out of here," she said. "I think they're searching down this way."

I stared at the bloody knife in my palm for a minute. I didn't know if Tyler was good or bad. I didn't know if he would live or die. But those women were innocent and they needed me now. Soon enough I had half the women free of their binds.

The other women stared at Tyler's limp form in a horrified awe that surpassed my own, as if it hadn't occurred to them that he was human like them. That's when I realized how well-trained these women were. Whatever their past was, in this moment, they knew themselves as slaves. They even looked at me that way, like I was some sort of Valkyrie warrior instead of just a used up whore.

"Do any of you know how to drive a boat?" I asked when all of them were loose.

Most of them stared back numbly, their eyes not even registering the question. I wasn't even sure how many of them spoke English, since they didn't seem to speak at all. The woman who I'd first freed said, "I think...maybe I saw it done...I could try." I couldn't detect an accent, although she seemed to stumble over the words.

"Good," I said, feigning confidence. "We have a captain."

We crossed the beach. A nervous energy sizzled through the air. The slaves weren't used to such freedom.

I wasn't used to anyone trusting me for anything.

The women trudged through the water to reach the rope ladder. I directed them up, warning them about the glass in the cabin. The woman who was going to drive the boat went up last. I looked back at Tyler, a dark lump on the sand, trying to figure out how to get him up on the boat.

The smallest splash was my only warning, as slight as a fish swishing at the surface. But it wasn't a fish. Not the hand clamped on my mouth, trapping my scream and blocking my air. Not the press of a cold metal barrel on my temple.

"Miss me?" Leo murmured beside my ear. I shuddered from the chill.

He pushed me through the ankle-deep water until we reached the beach. But when there was only a dark spot where Tyler's body had been. I glanced around wildly and found him leaning against a tree at the edge of the beach. He looked casual, when he shouldn't even have been able to stand. "Let her go, Leo."

"Don't come near us," Leo spat.

Tyler couldn't come near us at all, not with a gun pressed to my head. His hands were up, and words were coming out of his mouth, words about deals and staying calm and just take it easy, take a breath.

"You think I'm angry?" Leo asked. "I'm not angry. This is perfect. You and your little whore here did all the work for me, rounding up the slaves. Now all I have to do is ride away with them."

I flicked a glance over the boat. Several pairs of white eyes blinked at us from the shadows. It wouldn't be hard to figure out the situation here, even if they couldn't hear our words. They'd know their lives were at stake.

"Just think about it for a minute," Tyler said. "Ten slaves, that's a lot to handle. And there's just one of you. You need another pair of hands. I just want to help."

"Fuck that," Leo spat. "You want a cut of the pie. I'm sick and tired of sharing."

"No, man. Just want to help, that's all. I want to see this deal go right."

"Yeah, yeah, like this last deal worked out so great for me, with you and Carlos all cozy, and me in the hallway, babysitting the whore?"

"No, I'm trying to work something out here. That's all."

"Work something out?" Leo was shouting and shaking with what I recognized as fear. "We've got a boatload of fucking girls, and the cops are on their way."

"Calm down. Just calm down. I can talk to them."

"Fucking dirty cops—can't trust them! I think you and your cop friends want my girls, then you'll make me take the fall."

I didn't get to hear Tyler's response to that, because a rumble came from the boat as it came alive. In slow motion it shuddered in the water and turned out to sea with all the slaves.

"What the *fuck* just happened?" Leo asked incredulously.

"They were untied," I whispered, thinking that they'd signed our death sentence, thinking I was glad they were safe after all. I had done it. I had helped.

But then Leo wasn't behind me anymore. Tyler had him on the ground where they grappled to be on top. The gun glittered in a wide arc, reflecting gray moonlight at me, and landed a few yards from them. I went to grab it, but Leo and Tyler were in constant motion, flinging sand, and it was impossible to see. They rolled into the shallow water, but the moonlight was too little to judge Tyler's life by.

I held the gun with shaking hands, trying to get a shot. A hard grip grabbed my forearm, and I froze. Oh God, I hadn't noticed anyone sneaking up behind me. The cops? They'd arrest us all.

But it was worse than that.

"Mia." Carlos chuckled. "You little whore, always causing trouble."

Jesus, he almost sounded proud. I was definitely going to die. His thumb pressed a spot on my arm, and next thing I knew, my arm hung limply at my side and the gun was in his hands.

Bang.

Water shot out from the fighting figures, and one man slumped into the water. In gasping horror, I watched Tyler slowly stand up.

"Tyler," I cried.

"It's okay," he said to me, keeping his eyes trained on Carlos and his hands raised. But I knew it wasn't. He was about to die, about to be shot before my eyes. Desperate, I yanked Carlos's arm and twisted around until the barrel of the gun pointed in my stomach.

"Run," I called to Tyler, staring into Carlos's surprised eyes.

I heard the string of curse words he emitted that said he definitely was not running. Damn him.

Carlos sneered at me. "You actually want this asshole? The guy who tried to *buy* you, like you were a thing?"

That would sound bad to most people, I knew, but for Carlos it was pretty much the status quo. So actually, I didn't understand the big deal. Carlos must have read that in my eyes because he said, "I didn't buy you. I made you."

Carlos peered into my eyes, as if he were really seeing me. But even more disconcerting was the fact that I could see *him* like this, just a man. This must be how those slaves had looked at Tyler, how I looked at Carlos now. He was just a man, and a flawed one at that.

Then, just as quickly, the moment was over and he was back to his cold self. He pushed me, and I stumbled back into the water and into Tyler's arms. I thought we'd die like that, in each other's arms, like a tragedy fit for the stage. Tyler pushed me behind him.

"Go ahead and take her," Carlos said carelessly. "Consider her a gift, though I can't say if she's worth much."

He turned and walked away. I stared from around

Tyler, waiting for the punchline. Like Carlos would turn around and shoot us, laughing to himself about the poor saps who believed him for a second. Even after he disappeared into the woods, I blinked, unable to believe that I was free.

"Is he…is he serious?" I said.

"I think so," Tyler said, his voice thin and raspy. "Good. That's good."

Then he fell into the water, unable to even put his hands up to block his fall before he passed out. I turned him over so that at least his face was out of the water and dragged him onto the shore. Only then did I notice the dark stain at the front of his shirt. I lifted the hem and recognized the gash of a knife, similar to the one I had only this one wasn't for show. It was jagged and deep. He must have gotten it fighting with Leo.

I realized I was chanting, *Oh God, Oh God,* almost like a prayer.

"Shh," I heard. Tyler was looking at me through slitted eyes. "It will be okay. Go find Zachary."

"I can't leave you." I felt sure that if I left him, even to get help, he'd be dead before I returned.

"I have to tell you—"

"No, you don't have to explain." I wasn't sure I wanted to know.

"I should have sent you away at the beginning." His voice was threaded with pain, but underlaid with steel. He was using up all his words, all his strength, just for this. "I should have…I never should have walked away in the first place. I came back. I just had to get my mom out of here. It took me awhile to work it out, a couple of months, but when I came back, you were gone."

My breath left me in a soundless whoosh of air.

"I convinced myself that you'd gotten away safe, but you never did, did you? You've never been safe."

I couldn't answer.

"And then when I found you, Jesus. I was horrified, but at the same time, I couldn't let you go."

"God, Tyler."

"Go—" The word caught in his throat as he struggled to control the swath of pain that flitted across his face. His breath was coming faster, less even. "Be safe," he said, like a farewell.

"No," I half-shouted, half-sobbed.

Then the shadows of the beach splintered into the shapes of men. The cops ran at me, terrifyingly large. I didn't care that they'd arrest him or me, as long as they saved his life. "Please," I begged them as they knelt at his side. "Please help him."

Zachary was pulling me away from him. I fought him, but I was getting weaker, barely able to pull away, barely able to stand. The last dregs of strength I'd been using had finally failed me.

I looked up into Zachary's kind eyes. "Help him."

"We will. Just stay awake. Stay with me."

And maybe that's how I knew I was really released from Carlos's hold, that I was really free, because for the first time in a long time, I was disobedient. I fell into a deep slumber.

CHAPTER THIRTEEN

"**D**ON'T SCRATCH THEM," Tyler admonished. Healing wounds itched, which meant that three days later, I was unbearably itchy, all over my body.

I gave him a look that told him exactly what I thought of him giving me advice when he was the one who insisted on visiting me in the middle of the night. He was on complete bed rest, unlike me, who was technically allowed to get up and move around at will. But he'd shown up tonight, almost sheepish.

"I feel fine," he protested at my accusing look. "Besides, I needed to talk to you."

"You already explained everything." Most of it on the beach. Then the cops had explained the rest when I'd woken up, about how Tyler hadn't been an official informant, but he'd sent them information anyway. About how Tyler had been rescuing the women when I'd pulled my Xena Warrior Princess stunt and nearly killed the man.

"Not everything." He sat down on the white metal chair beside my hospital bed. Then he glanced back up. "You see, I just went in for you. I was only going to convince you to come with me and get you out of there."

He shook his head, bemused, disgusted, resigned. "But along the way, I got caught up in the cause. Zachary's cause. Your cause. Freeing those women."

He reached for my hand, and I let him take it.

"My mother was a whore," he said tightly. His shame arced between us through our clasped hands, another bond between us.

"Yeah," he said, and paused. "I couldn't let it go. I couldn't have walked away and leave these women here, even if it meant not saving you."

I didn't know what he was waiting for. "It's okay," I tried. "I understand."

"It's not okay," he bit out. "You almost died for that."

"Almost died to save those women? It would have been worth it. I'm not—"

"Don't say it," he interrupted savagely. "Don't say any of that. You're beautiful, you're smart. You're *alive*."

"Okay," I agreed, not really meaning it.

He rested his forehead on the back of my hand. "What can I do to prove it to you?"

I shook my head, though he couldn't see me. "It doesn't matter."

"It does, but we don't have to solve this tonight. Tomorrow you're getting discharged and so am I. I'd like it if you came and stayed with me, but if you want to get your own place..."

He went on for a few minutes, talking about plans that I'd never need. Then he left. I didn't think he fully trusted me, but he knew where I was at least, and he'd probably be back first thing in the morning.

I rattled in the frail hospital bed, restless for comfort that would be a long time coming. A whisper from the door snapped my attention away from my study of the ceiling tiles. The sky blue privacy curtain blocked my view, but I saw bare feet, too small to be Tyler's, make their way from the door and then pause.

"Who is it?" I whispered.

The metal rings rattled as the curtain was pushed aside. Stacey stood in the dim light from the moon and the instruments, swathed in a hospital-issue blanket.

"Do you mind?" she asked diffidently.

"No, come in." I waved her to the sofa and joined her there. Both of us wore hospital gowns, and huddled there while everyone around us slept, it felt like what I'd imagined a sleepover would be. Like having a best friend or a sister. I didn't know her, not even her last name, but I'd almost died with her.

"Have you…talked to anyone? From home?"

"Yeah." She pulled at a loose thread on the uneven gown stitching. "My husband is on his way from Idaho."

I tried to hide my surprise. Married. Jesus.

She gave me a small smile. "I don't know how that's going to work. I was in China for my job, a six month contract. Never made it past two weeks before I was taken." She fingered her blonde curls. "I guess I stood out there."

How ironic that they'd brought her back, almost

home but miles away. The words of comfort died on my tongue: *it will be okay* or *he'll understand.* I barely knew what "okay" looked like, and how the hell could he understand?

"So that's my story," she said, business-like. "What about you?"

I lowered my eyes in shame. "I wasn't like you. I was with Carlos."

"Carlos?"

"You know. Middle aged guy. Hispanic. In-charge. Always dressed nice." Compared to the other gangbangers, he stood out like a sore thumb. That was how he liked it.

She shook her head. "There were some Chinese guys who dressed well at the beginning, before we were shipped. But once we landed here, all we saw were the thugs who handled us. Well, and Tyler."

I looked up. "You know him?"

Her eyes softened. "Of course. He was always stepping in, telling them not to mess up the merchandise. Slipping extra food in our rations. I actually felt bad about hurting him, but I didn't know he was helping us escape."

She stared at the dark glass of the window, which only reflected the outline of the hospital room back at us, as her words taunted me with understanding. She hadn't ever seen Carlos there. I knew he hadn't spent a lot of time there. After all, he had been with me. But it seemed strange that he wouldn't visit at all, to check on his possessions, to train the girls, to make them suffer. Apparently I was the only girl to feel the bite of his belt.

Carlos gave me to Tyler. Not that I considered that any kind of binding agreement, but what did it mean? If I'd thought about it before all this, I would have said Carlos would kill me when he was finished with me. Yet he didn't. He gave me to a man who betrayed him.

We both should have died, but instead we lived, paired by a psychopathic matchmaker. Maybe it was just another mind fuck, getting to pull the strings on the puppets that were Tyler and I. But what kind of sadist orchestrated a happy ending?

"You're not going back to him are you?" Stacey asked, pulling me from my musings.

I laughed at myself, my gaze flicking over to the packed suitcase that had mysteriously arrived in my hospital room the day I woke up, along with two thousand dollars in cash. Blood money. "I got dumped, actually."

"Lucky girl," she said wryly.

No, luck had never done anything for me, but Carlos had given me that much. He had always taken care of me. Maybe he'd done plenty wrong, taking advantage of a homeless, underage girl, binding her to him through fear and shame, and causing her endless pain. But how could I forget that he had also saved me, that he protected me? He cared for me. The realization was like a final lash of his belt.

"Are you okay?" Stacey looked concerned.

"I'm fine," I assured her. "I think it's time to move on. Maybe I'm finally ready."

"Yeah? Well, don't leave me hanging. Tell me the secret."

"You don't want to follow in my footsteps. Trust me."

She smiled, and this time it touched her eyes. "You're going to be just fine."

She gave her email address to me, saying to keep in touch. I didn't have an email address, not having been allowed much computer time with Carlos. I accepted it with no intention of ever contacting her again, but I slipped the paper into my bag just in case. Inside the luggage, I found jeans and a conservative t-shirt that I could have sworn I hadn't owned before.

I poked my head out of the hospital room, half expecting a policeman or a militant nurse to berate me. But I was an adult, and I was not under arrest. My body was free, so why was it so hard for my mind to accept? A few figures shuffled through the halls, distracted doctors or blank-faced patients, but no one noticed me. I straightened my shoulders and rolled my luggage through the hallways, looking for all the world like a confident, normal woman.

Somewhere above me, in this very hospital, Tyler lay recovering from his stab wounds. The wound I'd given him. The wounds he'd gotten while trying to save me, to protect me. If I were a good woman, I would be in this room when he came for me. A good woman would nurture him, could love him. But I didn't know how to love, and the only thing I knew how to nurture was a cock to orgasm, repeatedly. I had nothing to offer Tyler, nothing he couldn't get from any corner girl. My pride wouldn't allow me to crawl to him like some stray puppy that Carlos had cast off.

I had survived my life with Carlos in a cocoon of pathetic gratefulness. I'd always found something to be grateful for, even under the whistle of a belt or within the confines of a cage. Yet now that I had everything, I couldn't find any thanks inside me at all. I was empty.

When the sliding doors opened, the smell of damp city air and smoke hit me in the face. I'd been a whore before I'd ever been a woman. Never safe, but always owned. I stepped into the fog, a free woman. I could do anything I wanted, but I would be alone.

I could go anywhere, but I had nowhere to go.

Chapter Fourteen

T HE HOUSE WAS smaller than I remembered. The yard, the neighborhood—everything was smaller. It was also dirtier and more run-down, though I didn't know if that was also the result of faulty memory or whether time had worked its ruinous magic.

No car sat in front of the house. Weeds had eaten up any grass from the yard. The door sat slightly unhinged. None of these things meant for sure that no one lived here. But a hush enveloped the house like a fog, probably warning away even the most desperate of slum-dwellers or delinquents.

Sure enough, when I poked at the front door, it creaked open. Dust swam through the air, little bugs illuminated by the bright sunlight—a hypochondriac's nightmare. I stepped inside.

The same red and green plaid couch slouched in the living room. The same knotty oak table sat in the small dining alcove. The same yellowed refrigerator leaned against the wall in the kitchen, absent of the rattle that indicated it was working.

I walked through the rooms with my hands tightly clasped, the way someone might view the wreckage of some disaster, curious but detached. Neither the furniture nor the years of dust held the answers to my childhood, not any more than the ancient oak trees could explain the wars or the greed of men. I hadn't come for the inside.

At the screen door, I looked out at the small, unkempt lawn. At that patch of dirt where an eighteen year-old-boy had once stood, making a request for mercy on behalf of a girl who couldn't speak for herself. That had been over ten years ago, ten years for guilt and frustration and anger to fester. Ten years to silently, privately rage against a monster in plain sight. A man who'd died seven years ago of a heart attack, according to the city records I'd found.

I was grateful that the tire still seemed so big. I crawled inside, not fitting as well as I had before, but still able to squish all my limbs inside. I understood the women who preferred the crushed enclosure of the hold to the freedom and the ocean spray. The world will toss you like the waves, heedless of your pain or your pleasure. Curled into the rubber tire, my whole world narrowed to the distant circle of sky.

No one ever looked for me here. No one ever cared to, except for one man.

I didn't sleep in that tire. I drifted away to the safe place where nothing could touch me.

Footsteps crunched the brittle weeds and world-worn pebbles, coming closer. I waited with bated breath. My sun was eclipsed by a dark head, shadowed so that I couldn't see who it was. I knew, though. I just knew.

"Hey, little girl."

I swallowed against the thickness. "You shouldn't be out of bed."

"You shouldn't be out here alone."

I allowed him to pull me out of the hole, and we sat side-by-side on the tire. Both of us were bigger physically. Both of us were stronger mentally. I'd read once about how swords were made in ancient times. They folded the metal over, each time melting it and reforming it into a new, stronger blade. That was me, and though he didn't see it that way, it was Tyler.

He crouched down before me, trailed a soft caress through my hair. "Tell me what you want." His eyes softened, as if he already knew. But he needed me to say it.

I shook my head, unseeing. If only it were that simple.

"You thought you could sneak out of the hospital and be done with me?" His finger on my chin turned my gaze to his. "You're mine."

I braved a laugh. "Just because Carlos said so. Because he *gave* me to you."

Tyler regarded me solemnly. "You were always mine. I was just too young and stupid to do anything about it." He shook his head slowly, regret plain on his face. "I left you."

"You were right to leave," I choked out. "I'm a…whore."

His grip tightened around the back of my neck. "No, Mia. You never were. Never."

This time my laugh was real and watery.

He shook his head in the face of my disbelief. "I failed you back then. I didn't know what I had. Didn't know how to protect you. Never again. I'm here now, and I'm not leaving, unless you want me to."

He sounded so sure. "What if I don't want you?"

A hoarse laugh. "I'm not even sure I could leave then. Tell me what you want, Mia."

You. I wanted things I'd never have. It was cruel of him to tease me this way.

"You're wrong. I am a whore." I had no money, nothing but my body to trade for food. I was back to where I'd been ten years ago in every sense of the phrase. *Tell me what you want,* he'd said. "I want money."

He shrugged, not bothered at all. "No problem."

I scrutinized him, trying to figure out what was up. "In exchange for my body."

An easy nod. "Fine."

Dammit, I couldn't read him. What was he playing at? He didn't really want someone like me, not in his real life. And that was the worst part of it. If he'd really been like Carlos or like Leo, he could have kept me. He would have kept me locked away. Only when I found out that he couldn't, he wouldn't ever do that no matter what he said, did I know for sure that was what I wanted.

A normal man, an honorable one, had no business with me.

"Let's go," he said. "You didn't keep Carlos waiting, did you?"

I frowned, almost positive he was teasing. A light flickered in his brown eyes, warming them, but his lips were flat, deadpan. "I'm serious. We have a deal."

"Are you sure? You haven't even set a price yet." He smiled slightly. "I don't think you're very good at this."

I flushed, the bastard. Definitely teasing.

Even worse, he was right. I knew nothing about the business of whoring. I'd made a few deals on the streets before Carlos, mostly for food. I'd met a few who serviced Carlos's men, but they didn't stay long enough to get close. And Carlos himself hadn't played much with other women when I had been there, maybe never. How had I never realized that before, how odd it was for a man like him? Faithfulness.

I had no idea how much a whore should charge. I thought back to that movie, Pretty Woman. Didn't she charge $700 for the week? That had included room and board. But that was a long time ago. There was inflation to consider. Or did whores not count for inflation? Damn him for making this difficult.

"A thousand dollars a week," I finally said.

He didn't laugh but considered it. "So that's—what? About fifty thousand a year? Done."

I blinked. Had he just hired me…full time?

He had me by the hand and was pulling me toward the dark car parked out front, then he stopped and cocked his head toward the house. "Was there anything you wanted from here?"

I looked back at it, peeling paint, sagging porch, broken windows and all. "No."

His hand tightened, and I looked over. "I own it."

I sucked in a breath. "Why?"

He shrugged, looking vaguely guilty. "When your dad died, it went up for auction. You were long gone by then, but I guess I thought you might come back someday...or maybe I just didn't want anyone else to live there."

His words flooded me with warmth. It was a fucked-up bond we shared, twisted and gnarled like the arteries gripping a heart, but it was real. He knew me.

"I don't want anyone else to live there either. I want—" It was still hard to do this, to say what I wanted. I swallowed years of training. "I want it to be torn down."

His eyes shone with something I could have sworn was pride. "Consider it done."

"Thank you." The emotions spilled over, threatening to drown out the sense of peace that had embraced me ever since I'd walked out of the hospital a free woman.

Maybe he knew how much this meant to me, how close I was to the edge, because he added, "But I'm taking it out of your wages."

A smile tugged at my lips, but I hid it with my hand. He really was a bastard.

He took me by surprise, pulling my hand away and pressing a kiss to my lips. Just as quickly, he straightened.

His eyes smiled, even if he didn't.

"Come on," he said. "We have a busy day."

Then he proceeded to make good on his threat by taking me to store after store. I'd never shopped much at all, not with my dad, certainly. And Carlos had usually bought my clothes for me, ordering what he wanted me to wear. Dressing me like a doll. Tyler was the same way, insisting I buy clothes and lots of them. Except I had to pick out everything. I wanted freedom, but this overwhelmed me. Just when I was sure I'd had enough, Tyler took me to his house.

A little cottage-style home beamed at me from its small lot. I didn't belong here.

I flashed guilty glances at the rows of oak trees as we went up the sidewalk. I knew Tyler noticed, but thankfully, he didn't comment.

He ordered pizza, saying he only cooked mac and cheese and I was too worn out to do it. Then he turned on a movie, some romantic comedy rental that I stared at in utter shock and awe. The whole evening left me dazed, like I'd stepped into a fantasy land. Almost like I was a regular person.

I took a long shower. Well, not that long. I'd found one thing I missed from my life with Carlos—God, had it only been a week ago that I'd lived in his compound?—the endless supply of hot water. Even the hospital, where I'd had to stay the past week, had a good supply. In this small house, with only a bachelor to break it in, the water heater tapped out in ten minutes.

It was comforting to find something wrong with this picture, as if it might not be a dream after all. When I came out of the bathroom, Tyler was leaning in the corner, watching me.

I wanted things back on solid ground, so I dropped my towel. I heard his quick inhale, but he didn't move. He'd watched before at Carlos's place, so I went to the dresser and brushed out my hair.

I knew he was trying to do some kind of savior shit with all this. Like maybe I'd go to sleep a whore and wake up tomorrow a normal woman. The mirror reflected my naked body, with pink scars and yellowish bruises blooming across my skin. I looked like an unfinished art project, painted with fists. The abuse was etched into my skin, branding me forever as a whore. It was better that he see this, that he not forget.

When I'd pulled the brush through the wet strands enough times, I put down the brush, watching the man approach me through the mirror. His eyes were on mine, but of course he could see me in all my lack of glory. That probably explained the lust in his eyes. If he'd thought I was that little girl back at the house, I'd reminded him what I was now.

He didn't disappoint. With his hands on my hips and his mouth on my neck, he pulled me flush against him. And just to dispel any doubt, a hard bulge pressed into my lower back. I closed my eyes and let my head fall back, knowing his body would be there to catch me.

"I thought you might hold off," I murmured.

His breath blew hot against my skin, damp from his tongue. "Hold off why?"

"You know." I wiggled my backside against his erection, earning a groan for my trouble. "Trying to be honorable or something."

He nipped my earlobe. "I'm not honorable."

My eyes opened and met his in the mirror. "I think you are."

His brown eyes flashed, light reflecting his denial. "Like you think you're a whore?"

"You're going to pay me, aren't you? And you're going to fuck me, won't you?"

His cock prodded me intimately. "I'll give you my money." He plunged inside, I gasped. "I'll give you everything I have." And again, deeper. "Everything I am." His lips touched my ear as he whispered, "And yes, I'm going to fuck you. All the time."

Then he was pulling out and thrusting back inside, filling me and turning me inside out. I held onto the dresser, fingers gripping tight like at the edge of a cliff, but it was too late, I was already falling. I'd fallen for him years ago.

He straightened his body, angling his cock higher on every thrust. Pleasure built, spiraling higher. The dresser melted away and my shame faded to nothing. There were only his labored breaths against my nape and his cock inside me. I crashed into my orgasm with violent shudders and an ache where my cold heart used to be.

He deepened his thrusts, working my body for his

own release. I watched his face in the mirror, fierce with intention and slack with arousal. I knew when he came, not just from the fingers tight on my hips, grinding me down, or the hot pulse inside me, but from the glimpse of ecstasy on his face.

We stumbled together to the bed, collapsing in a sated heap of cotton sheets and cooling sweat. My eyes were closed, but I could feel him, unmoving. His hand found mine, and I latched onto him.

"There's a different name for that, Mia. When a man gives a woman everything he has. When a man fucks a woman. All the time."

My breath caught. "Marriage?"

"You're a greedy little one," he said on a laugh. "I was going to say love."

I jabbed him in the side. "And you're a sap."

He pushed up onto his elbow. "So marry me."

I hid my wide smile in his chest, trying to contain the elation that threatened to burst me into tears.

"Don't tease me," he warned. "Tell me your answer."

I did him one better. I showed him.

EPILOGUE

I KNEW WHAT hunger felt like, claw marks in my belly. I knew what pain and fear felt like. My body still had the marks. Happiness felt foreign. Peace, even more so.

Dappled sunlight on my face.

Green grass spongy between my toes.

A warm hand holding mine.

There was a sense of timelessness, as if I could sit here forever. As if I already had. The porch wasn't broke down and grim. It was freshly painted white with honeysuckle just starting to twine around the railing. And instead of a tire swing, there was a hammock— woven fabric with colorful stripes.

I'd fallen asleep in that hammock, cradled in the arms of my lover. I'd woken up confused, disoriented, and toppled us both out of the net. I still remember Tyler's laugh, the timbre of it, the vibration it made through my body, like a mark that can't be seen.

"Mia?" he asked softly.

He did that a lot—called me back. I look at our hands linked together. "I'm okay."

He squeezed my fingers gently. "You don't have to pretend for me."

Sometimes I just didn't know if it was possible. How could the marks of hunger and pain fade away? It had been years since I'd been on the streets, years that I'd been in Carlos's care, and they were as fresh as ever.

"I can't..." My throat tightened, and I had to stop. Tyler waited until I could speak again. "I can't forget."

From inside the house, his cellphone rang.

He swore softly. "Ignore it."

"No." I begged him with my eyes. "Answer it."

After another couple rings, he cursed again and went to answer it.

For the first month, he had refused to leave my side. He'd made a cocoon for us here, a safe place for us to rest. And I needed to know that we could emerge anew and spread our wings. He may not admit it, but he needed to be back out there working for the FBI as much as they needed him.

I blinked as a small light flashed from the tree line where the yard turned into woods. My heart beat a little faster. Sometimes it felt like I was being watched. Like I was being watched over.

Carlos. My own perverted guardian angel.

The FBI would never find him, that much I was sure of. Hesitantly, I waved at the trees, and whoever might be behind them. Then felt incredibly silly. For one thing Tyler had set up excellent security around the property. Although if anyone could get past it, it was Carlos.

But Carlos had let me go. I meant nothing to him. No, that wasn't quite true. We'd had something, even if it wasn't love.

Even if it wasn't forever.

The porch wood creaked behind me. Tyler stepped up and pressed a kiss to my forehead before he sat.

"Your supervisor?" I asked.

"Not yet, he isn't," he muttered. "Doesn't stop him from giving orders."

I smiled a little. Oh, he wanted to go back. "You didn't tell him yes?"

"When I'm ready."

"When *I'm* ready, you mean." He'd stay here forever if I let him. "I told you I'm fine."

"Mia," he said in warning.

"It's because of my nightmares," I whispered, re-signed. I couldn't hide them from him. He'd woken me up, my throat hoarse from screaming.

He shook his head. "Not only yours, Mia. I have nightmares too," he said, his voice hushed like he was giving a confession. Like the shaded backyard was a church. Like he needed to repent. "I have nightmares where we're back there, and I don't know how to protect you. Or worse—where you're gone, and I can't find you."

It shook me, that he'd admit that. He was a strong man. Physically. Emotionally. He didn't have any weakness that I could see, but he was afraid...for me. I reached for him then, using my hands to soothe him. I would have used my mouth too, but I was learning to give comfort without sex.

I rested my forehead against his shoulder.

"That's why I keep you close," he said. "Maybe too close. I don't want you to feel like you're trapped here."

The porch swing creaked softly in the wind. A dog barked in the distance, probably the beagle who lived two doors down. It should have been sweet and soft. In my dreams, in my wildest wishes, that was how it had been, muted with clouds and lace.

This wasn't soft.

It was hard—an ache in my breastbone and rough wood against my thighs. It was the haunted look in Tyler's eyes, a pain I could never quite soothe with my body.

"Trap me," I said, looking straight at him, facing the pain head-on. "Forever."

The darkness eased, just slightly. Pleasure flickered in those dark eyes, so familiar and yet so far away. I saw the promise in his eyes, the carnality, and prepared myself to get on my knees, right there on the porch steps in front of him.

Please don't take me up to the bedroom. I wanted to be used, not wrapped in muslin and put away.

"Lay back." His voice had gone hard.

I leaned back on my elbows first, feeling the cotton of my dress catch on the wood. The thin fabric provided little cushion as I draped myself over the top step.

He was the one who knelt at the bottom, in front of me. He smoothed my dress up my legs and rested one hand inside my thigh. His gaze met mine. "I love you,

Mia. You're mine. Always."

Tears filled my eyes and slid down the side of my face. "Tyler."

Then his hands were pushing my thighs apart. The summer breeze felt impossibly cold against my exposed cunt, bare and naked. His lips were a shock, hot and agile and knowing. And his tongue—God, his tongue— slick and hot. I rocked my hips up to meet him, but he pressed me back down, pressed my hips into the wood.

"Stay, baby," he murmured against my clit. "Stay still for me."

I tried. I tried so hard to do what he asked of me. It was such a small request, but I struggled with it, trembled with the effort it took to keep my body flat on the porch steps. The step cut into my back, but that wasn't where I really hurt. Lower, lower. I wanted to reach for him, to beg for him, when all he wanted me to do was *stay*.

All my life I had been able to do this. *Lie there and take it.* But now it was my greatest challenge, almost painful, as my clit throbbed and my skin tingled all over.

"Please," I mumbled. "Please, please."

He didn't answer. He just wrapped his large hands around my thighs to hold me down—*trapping me*, exactly as I'd asked him to—and lashed my clit with his tongue. He sucked at my cunt with his mouth and scraped along the edge with his teeth. He made me cry and shudder. He made me scream and beg.

It was too harsh and rough and painful—until he

reached up and took my hand. Then I could squeeze him just as hard as I needed. Then I wasn't alone.

A warm hand holding mine.

Green grass spongy between my toes.

Dappled sunlight on my face.

And the hot warmth of his tongue as he pushed me into climax again and again. He ran his face over my thighs, against my belly, spreading my arousal everywhere, as if he couldn't touch enough of me. Every time I came, his low groan of male satisfaction rent the air.

At one time I didn't even know what happiness felt like. But I was pretty sure it couldn't be better than this.

THE END

THANK YOU!

Thank you for reading Trust in Me! I hope you enjoyed Tyler and Mia's story.

- Meet the woman who brings Carlos to his knees in Don't Let Go.

- Would you like to know when my next book is released? You can sign up for my newsletter at skyewarren.com/newsletter.

- Like me on Facebook at facebook.com/skyewarren.

- I appreciate your help in spreading the word, including telling a friend.

- Reviews help readers find books! Leave a review on your favorite book site.

- Turn the page for an excerpt from Don't Let Go...

Don't Let Go

"Beautiful. Poignant. Complex. Haunting."

—Leila DeSint, author of the London Brown series

Junior FBI Agent Samantha Holmes is assigned the case of a lifetime, along with an enigmatic new partner, Ian Hennessy. She's determined to prove herself to the bureau legend, but late nights and stolen moments lead to more than respect. They lead to desire, and soon she's fallen for the one man forbidden.

Together they hunt for the FBI's most wanted man. A criminal. A psychopath. But when they get close, Samantha may end up prey instead. She must face her dark past to stay alive—and to protect the man she loves.

"The chemistry between these two burns hot. The heat they create is utterly, darkly seductive. Combined with the emotions behind it, watching these two souls, broken beyond repair, find an unusual solace in each other... enthralling. Erotic. Breathtaking."

–Romantic Book Affairs

EXCERPT FROM DON'T LET GO

HENNESSY CUT A striking form against the window's glow, but the silver streaking his honey-brown hair at his temples proved he was older than me. Much older, in both years and experience. Despite the obvious differences between my new partner and me, it felt good to be part of the club. A sense of contentment and happiness swelled inside me. However it had come about, this gig would lift me out of the professional gutter in a way that coffee runs and paper filing had never done.

The door closed me in with an audible click. My walk across the carpet, however, didn't make a sound. Years of rigorous training, both inside the academy and out, had left me as agile as any practiced field agent. Still, I felt sure he tracked my every movement, effortlessly, with the kind of awareness born of experience. How long had he been an agent? Ten years, twenty? Criminals had shot at him, tried to blow him up, paid money to assassinate him. Any agent with a resume like his would have been a target. His survival gave testament to his skill.

Eyes the color of sheet metal stared at the window,

unseeing. Small imperfections marred a handsome face: a slight curve of his nose where it had broken, a small scar on his chin. A line of white scar tissue split a brown eyebrow. He'd done more than evade these criminals; he'd fought them.

"You should've taken him up on his offer," he said quietly.

My boss, he meant. Had he heard the low conversation we'd exchanged? Or did he just deduce what was being said? *If you want out, tell me now.*

"I'm not interested in his offer. I want this case."

"You have no idea what this case is even about, rookie."

Questions sat on the tip of my tongue. *So what's the case about, then? When can we get started?* But only one came out.

"What happened to the last guy?"

That finally got his full attention. He looked at me, and I felt the gaze of his gunmetal eyes like a blow. It stole my breath and rendered me speechless. He looked me up and down. His mouth set in a flat line, unimpressed by my gender, my youth, or maybe the pink blouse I wore. Whatever he saw, it made him answer.

"He died. The last time I went after Carlos Laguardia, my partner died. A punk kid who thought he could bring down a monster."

His words and his tone challenged me. *Run away,* they said. But I heard the desolation beneath the warning. Whatever family or friends the *punk kid* might have had, this man had mourned him. Hennessy might be a ruthless agent, but he cared about his partners.

I extended my hand. "Then let's get the bastard responsible."

His eyes widened minutely, the faintest indication I'd surprised him before the cynical mask snapped back into place. He studied me, gauging my sincerity, my intelligence, or whatever resemblance I might have borne to the punk kid. I could see him judging my pearl earrings and the unfortunately youthful button nose on my face and finding me lacking. Most guys assumed I couldn't fight. I had my second Dan in Tae Kwon Do, and I was a better shot than the rest of my graduating class. I was freaking competent, and if this guy was going to question it, if he was going to be prejudiced and—

He nodded. Curtly. Decisively. His approval washed over me, warming me in a way that even Brody's hadn't. This guy was the real deal, the Lone Ranger of the country's gangland, and I'd gladly be his trusty sidekick.

He accepted my hand and awareness rose from where his skin heated mine. Awareness that he was a man, that he was a handsome one. I sensed an answering ripple go through him, as if he'd just registered me as a woman. Attraction, plain and simple. A chemical reaction, really.

I pushed it aside.

Besides that, a different kind of alertness had begun to move through me, one that had nothing to do with the lean muscled body in front of me. This assignment was real. The biggest case to come through our branch in the time I'd been here, and I'd just been assigned as a principal agent. Holy shit. I carefully schooled my expression, forcing back the giddiness. I didn't even care about whatever ulterior motives they might have had.

For surely there had been ulterior motives. A hundred other agents were more qualified for the role on this floor alone. It didn't matter. If I contributed one tiny thing that led to us bringing down Laguardia, I'd make a name for myself. No more schlepping coffee or making copies. But my desire ran even deeper than that. Even darker. The sinister excitement I'd felt when I'd held my father's life in my hands, when I'd turned him in—I felt it now too. It hummed through me, sleek and dark in my veins.

"What are we going to do first?" I asked Hennessey, my voice coming out breathless. I hoped he didn't notice the flush on my cheeks or my rapid pulse of excitement. The way his gaze flicked to the base of my neck and then away said my hope was in vain.

"First, you're going to study the case files. I'm already familiar, so I'll go ahead and do the questioning."

"Questioning?"

"An inmate. They're holding him down at the courthouse for his arraignment, and I need to speak with him."

A shiny laminate "Visitor" badge was clipped to his lapel. Despite his impressive credentials and senior rank, he was an outsider in this office. As a rookie, so was I.

"We," I corrected.

"Pardon?"

"*We* need to speak with him. I've already read the case files. I *do* know what this case is about. And I'm coming with you."

He radiated suspicion, as if he'd never heard of initiative and had never seen anyone be assertive. "Why would you read case files if you didn't know you'd get assigned here?"

"Because I ran out of money to buy more detective novels. Why do you think?" I blew out a breath, shocked at myself. What the hell? Being sarcastic wasn't the way to make friends. Then again, there was little chance of Hennessey being my friend. He didn't want me as a partner. He barely registered my existence.

Though, he registered me now. His eyes narrowed, his lips firmed. He wasn't happy, but I couldn't be sorry. His gray eyes took my measure, as more than an annoying new girl, as more than a woman—as an equal. "So you feel confident with the case? With Laguardia?"

"Yes, sir."

"State his full name."

"Carlos Frederico Laguardia." I continued to recite the next ten most commonly used aliases. We had no idea what his real birth name had been. Even his identity was a fabrication, a fraud like the disguises and the pretend trips.

If I'd expected Hennessey to be impressed with my recitation, I'd have been disappointed. He frowned. "Where was he last seen?"

"Switzerland." I paused, wondering how much I should say. How much to reveal to a partner who didn't yet trust me. "At least, that's what the official reports say. But it wasn't him."

One brow rose. "Explain."

His stern command sent a shiver down my spine. That autocratic tone annoyed me, but I couldn't deny he'd earned the right to use it. He had so much more experience, more skills than I. Where did I get off telling him he was wrong? Still, I'd pulled the lever to my own trap door by opening my mouth. The only thing left to do was fall through it.

I thought back to the world map pinned on the wall, the pins in all the reliable sightings, the yarn connecting them loose and drooping to the floor like streamers in a party long over.

"He doesn't like the cold," I finally said.

The silence grew thick and potent. "He doesn't like the cold?"

I shifted uncomfortably. "He avoids it. His head-quarters have always been in warm locations. Mexico. South America. The one in North Africa."

"The Algerian compound was never confirmed. And Mexico... South America... It didn't occur to you that those are the major centers of drug and weapons trafficking?" He looked incredulous.

"And Russia," I said quietly. My chest felt tight. I wished I'd never started this. "Russia is another major center of drug and weapon trafficking, but he never goes there." *Because it's cold.*

He stared at me as if I'd lost my mind. And maybe I had. Maybe that had happened years ago and neither the court-appointed psychiatrist nor the FBI staff who'd cleared me for duty had ever noticed.

Hennessey barked a laugh. "Jesus. You know, the Russians prefer human trafficking these days, having more people than drugs or weapons. And maybe Laguardia just doesn't like the Gulag. But I take your point." He laughed again, as if in disbelief. "It's a fair theory, and a new one, I'll give you that much."

The knot loosened inside me, letting me breathe again. He might suspect I was crazy, but at least he knew I paid attention. I could be an asset to him.

A new, grudging respect lightened his eyes, turning them silver. "Okay, rookie, you can come. But I'm driving."

I didn't bother hiding my smile. I didn't care who drove, and besides, that was to be expected. I doubted this man ever gave up much control. I bet his commands extended into the bedroom. The thought filled me with unexpected, unwelcome heat.

Want to read more? Don't Let Go is available at Amazon.com, BarnesAndNoble.com, and iBooks.

OTHER BOOKS BY SKYE WARREN

Wanderlust

On the Way Home

Hear Me

Prisoner

Dark Nights Series

Keep Me Safe (prequel)

Trust in Me

Don't Let Go

The Beauty Series

Beauty Touched the Beast

Beneath the Beauty

Broken Beauty

Beauty Becomes You

The Beauty Series Compilation

Standalone Erotic Romance

His for Christmas

Take the Heat: A Criminal Romance Anthology

Sweetest Mistress

Below the Belt

Dystopia Series

Leashed

Caged

About the Author

Skye Warren is the New York Times and USA Today Bestselling author of dark romance. Her books are raw, sexual and perversely romantic.

Sign up for Skye's newsletter:
www.skyewarren.com/newsletter

Like Skye Warren on Facebook:
facebook.com/skyewarren

Follow Skye Warren on Twitter:
twitter.com/skye_warren

Visit Skye's website for her current booklist:
www.skyewarren.com

ACKNOWLEDGEMENT

Thanks to my wonderful critique partners and beta readers: Leila DeSint, K.M., Bibliopolist and Jennifer Lowery. Also thanks to my editors, Helen Hardt and Em Petrova. The light you all shone on my dark imaginings has made them fit for public enjoyment.

COPYRIGHT

Made in the USA
Columbia, SC
25 April 2020

94192613R00109